THE HOUND AND THE PEACOCK

A FUC ACADEMY STORY

SCARLET FOX

ACKNOWLEDGMENTS

Thank you to Eve for letting us write in her world and use her setting and characters. It's always a fun project and amazing opportunity! I can't thank you enough.

Thank you to Jessica Ripley for all the sprints and advice for this book. She had the idea of Cass trying to move on from a traumatic incident that left her with physical scars in addition to mental ones.

Thank you to Rebecca Poole for the awesome cover art! I always find them delightful and cute.

And thank you Devin Govaere for the edits and suggestions for making this book shine.

1

———

Agent Cassandra Sparks couldn't believe she volunteered to work with Agent Grayson Stone again.

The Avian Soaring Security and the Furry United Coalition—ASS and FUC—never mixed well. Though Cass and Grayson's last mission in Toronto back in 2012 ended well—in a manner of speaking— both agents had vowed to never speak to each other again. At the time, both agencies were new, and Cass and Grayson wanted to prove themselves valuable assets. In that, they succeeded. They'd caught their bad guy, but they were at each other's throats by the end of it. That *was* Cass' fault. She cringed at the memory of telling Grayson he'd have to "eradicate the hick" in himself to be her boyfriend. Ouch.

The Cass back then stuck with Grayson for the great sex but worried what people back home would say. She wouldn't have been the first avian to opt for a mammal, but it would have been particularly difficult to justify Grayson to her persnickety flock. He didn't have "the look," as her mother would say, with his penchant for wearing cowboy hats and boots all the time. Cass' mother would take one head-to-toe glance in his direction and the squawking would begin... and probably never end. Mother could be a tad overbearing, a worried mother-hen. And the more upset she was, the shrilled her voice became.

Mother had always wanted Cass to settle down in a traditional home, hoped she'd choose a harem for herself. Unfortunately, Cass found the idea nauseating. She'd never enjoy being one of a handful of peahens who fell in line behind an attention-starved peacock. Living the life of a party—a group of peafowl—was not her idea of a good time. If Cass was going to lay eggs for any man, she was going to have him all to herself.

For a while, she'd actually thought Grayson was going to be that man. She just needed to clean him up a little. Put a little polish on the hound. Make him just a smidge more presentable.

How laughable she'd been back then. Not only for thinking that changing his wardrobe would make the party accept him but also for believing that the loyal and honest canine would be up for a makeover. Grayson was nothing if not true to himself, unable to pretend he was anything else. Asking him to change

—no, make that *demanding* he change—had been telling him he wasn't good enough. That he didn't deserve her love.

What a bitch she'd been.

She only understood that now, though, after she'd had to walk through the depths of hell and back.

During an ASS mission, Cass had been following a suspect in a highspeed car chase when she was hit with a bioweapon specifically made to target shifters. It not only caused her to crash into a utility pole, wrapping her car around it at over 100 km per hour, but the chemicals leached into her system, inhibiting her shifter regeneration abilities and leaving her to heal at a snail's pace. She didn't know how humans dealt with it. Even now, a mere papercut took a week to heal.

The accident had changed her views about essentially *everything*. It opened her eyes to how petty she was. Not at first. No, right after the incident, it felt like her world was crumbling. In fact, she had considered ending it, putting herself out of her misery and suffering. She'd been led to believe that, without her looks, she was a plucked bird. No one wanted to see that. Or at least, that's the image her mother reinforced with her incessant chirping. *"You'll never grace the stage again for another beauty pageant!"* was what her mother wailed at the side of Cass' hospital bed.

While Cass had been processing everything,

trying to embrace gratitude for being *alive*, her mother's world still revolved around how everyone looked and what they wore. *"Eww, those shoes were so last season,"* her mother would say about an offending pair of heels. Or, *"That dress does* nothing *for her figure."* She was relentless and brutal. Mother would find something wrong with practically everyone.

And those damned beauty contests. From a young age, Cass was thrown into child pageants, practically learning to walk in heels as a toddler. But the pageants didn't only teach her that beauty and grace were everything, they also molded her into someone with a cutthroat competitive side. As her mother would say, *"If you don't come in first place, then you didn't win."*

While it may not have served her in every aspect of life, that way of thinking had certainly helped her as she fought to overcome her injuries and get back to her life. She had to at least be thankful to her mother for giving her that.

Cass was lucky to be alive, but it didn't feel like that at first. She'd been stuck in Hell, looking at a reflection that wasn't her own. Trapped in a body that wouldn't move as she wanted. Now, as she stood in front of the bathroom mirror, getting ready for the day, she knew that many other people in accidents such as hers didn't live to talk about it. Cass might have scars on her face, but she could cover them with foundation, as she now did, carefully blending so that the freckles she had come to love were still visible. She'd come a long way since right after the incident, when her face was covered in stitches and bandages because a malfunction had prevented the airbag from deploying. Her cheek had been crushed when her face impacted with the steering wheel, and the doctors had grafted a portion of bone from her left hip onto her cheekbone to reconstruct her face.

Thank gods for medical advancements and technology.

She brushed on her eyeshadow and plopped on a set of fake lashes. After applying red lipstick that matched the cool, rosy undertones of her medium-brown skin, she preened in the mirror. It probably seemed silly to others, and maybe even the opposite of her "beauty isn't everything" revelation, but Cass still enjoyed makeup. After the reconstructive surgeries, it had helped to bring her back to life, in a way. At first, makeup was a comfort, hiding the scars to forget the terrible crash that marred her body. Makeup could change the way people looked at her, the way she felt. Eventually, though, she learned she didn't *need* makeup, but if she still wanted to use it, that was okay too. It was artwork; a choice. And it was one aspect of her hectic life that she could control. That much she'd learned when she'd been stuck in the hospital bed and her friend Bianca would bring a wide selection of polishes in so Cass could pick a color and Bianca would paint her nails. It was a small choice she controlled, but it made a difference.

Now, she rubbed some coconut leave-in conditioner on her curly hair to help keep her unruly red locks tame, giving them an extra fluff as she admired her crown. The new Cass had worked herself up from rock bottom, learning that beauty wasn't everything, which had been a difficult thing for a peacock shifter—and past beauty pageant winner—to recognize and accept. For all the days and months when she *couldn't* do her hair, she'd learned that it hadn't made a difference in who she truly was. She'd had to find confidence and value in herself without the outer wrapper and discover that true beauty wasn't what was on the surface; it was what was inside that really counted. A cliché most learned at a young age, but it hadn't been in her mother's book of childhood lessons.

She slipped on her favorite pair of rhinestone-encrusted stiletto heels, smiling as they sparkled in the sunlight that streamed through her window. Okay, maybe everything about her hadn't changed after the accident. If anything, three months in bed—"non-weight-bearing" as the doctors put it—with a broken pelvis had given her plenty of time to dream about shoes. So had the following weeks of learning to walk again when she was only allowed to wear sensible orthopedic shoes. Almost a year went by before Cass could walk without a limp and return to wearing her favorites.

It had been longer than that for her to accept her new reflection and become a warrior who was proud of her scars, who looked at them as a testament to how far she'd come.

Would Grayson notice she'd changed? When his name came through on a request from FUC to ASS, Cass had insisted she handle it personally. At first, she couldn't believe it. She'd kept tabs on Grayson and knew that he'd retired from the field to become a full-time instructor at FUCN'A—the Furry United Coalition Newbie Academy—but it appeared he was getting back into the action now that his students had been targeted in a kidnapping attempt.

FUC had only wanted help in identifying the red-tailed hawk shifter who'd been involved in the event, but Cass had other ideas. She jumped on the chance to head to Canada and work with Grayson on the case. Whenever avians were involved, ASS had a right to demand FUC let them in on the mission, whether they liked it or not. She had no idea how to patch things up with Grayson or prove that she was different than the woman he once knew, but working with him for the first time in over a decade seemed a good place to start.

Cass picked her cell phone up and dropped it inside her designer handbag. She slung its leather straps over her shoulder. After adjusting her hot-pink pencil skirt, she waltzed out the door of her room at the local bed and breakfast to head to WANC—the Working and Administration Networking Core— which was the main building on the FUCN'A campus. The Furry United Coalition Newbie Academy was where all the new cadets were trained to be proficient FUC agents. Who didn't want to be a talented FUC?

She'd surprised Grayson by showing up in his office the night before. She hadn't been sure what she'd expected, but she supposed having him insist they set up an official meeting for the next day was reasonable.

As she opened the door to her candy-apple-red sports car, the summer sun glistened on her glossy nails with the rhinestones embedded in them. Okay, maybe Cass still enjoyed flashy things a bit too much, but she could think of worse vices to be a slave to. Besides, weren't people always saying, "Do what makes you happy"? Cass felt glitter and glam did just that for her. She hunted down bad guys while looking fabulous, and last she checked, there was no rule against that.

Happy memories of the time she spent with Grayson sent her heart fluttering, but they faded behind the visions of her last fight with him. How she'd wronged him. She hoped he wouldn't be misguided by her fancy exterior and would see she'd matured. This assignment gave her the chance to accomplish that. But there were other obstacles as well. FUC had an abrasive relationship with ASS. They'd be starting off on the wrong paw and claw. She hoped Grayson could see this peahen had changed her feathers. Figuratively anyway.

2

Grayson paced the meeting room, fearing he'd wear a hole in the soles of his cowboy boots. Cass was late. As usual. She probably got distracted staring at her reflection. Or couldn't decide what pair of heels to wear.

He'd already been worked up about the case. His students had been under attack, targeted by an evil scientist. Dr. Smith's body had been recovered, but his accomplice, a red-tailed hawk shifter, was still at large.

Alyce Cooper, director of FUCN'A, had been ready to take his report and send it off to a FUC field office for them to handle. That wasn't good enough for Grayson. He knew how things like that went. FUC had bigger fish to fry, and they'd never get to this one, which meant, if he wanted to ensure the hawk was hunted down and captured, he had only one choice: pick up the case himself. Go back to the field after years of happy retirement.

Then *she* appeared. Showed up in his office looking as beautiful and smelling as alluring as ever. ASS Agent Cass Sparks. The peacock shifter who'd pecked his heart out. Two opposites who'd never had any business trying to be together. As he'd once said, he was grit and steel while Cass was equally fluff and sparkles.

"What are you doing here, Sparks?"

"What do you think I'm doing here? This is ASS business."

"The hell it is. They came after two of my *students. I am hunting that rat with wings down."*

"You're not off the case. I'm just on it, too."

It didn't matter how he felt about it—about *her.* He had to focus on the mission. He was about to call her when he sensed her arrival. Something in the air changed, as it always felt with her. As though everything else in the world stood still when Cass was in the vicinity.

She didn't say a word, didn't make a sound as she walked into the meeting room, quiet as a mouse. He'd never learned her secret on sneaking up on people while wearing stilettos. A peek at her feet confirmed she still wore them. Of course she did. Some things never changed.

He flicked his gaze up, taking in her bright pink pencil skirt and matching blazer. She looked more like a fashion magazine executive than a field agent, but that was Cass. A glittering pair of earrings peeked through her curly locks, flashing and catching his attention. His Basset Hound senses picked up on the coconut scent of her hair mingled with her sweet perfume. She smelled delicious. He stopped his mind from wandering as the lingering aroma brought him back to the last time he'd tasted her luscious body.

Snap out of it. "You know, Agent Sparks, only peacocks are colorful. Peahens are kind of plain." His voice came out dry, sarcastic even. He wanted his words and tone to demonstrate to Cass exactly where she stood. It was tough seeing her after so long. Back in Toronto, her comments had cut him deep, leading him to vow he'd never allow another person the power to leave him feeling not good enough.

To break his heart.

Commenting on her clothing choice was a direct reference to the conversation that had ended it all between them.

"I want to meet your mother," Grayson had said.

Cass, who'd always looked calm and confident, suddenly stiffened. Her eyes wide, she informed him, "I really don't think that's a good idea."

"Why not? I know I'm a hound and birds don't quite like my kind, but I'm pretty good at getting people to

like me."

She pursed her lips together. "I... I just can't allow it. Not unless you change your wardrobe and style."

He laughed it off, not taking her suggestion seriously. "What's wrong with the way I look?" He'd dressed that way his entire life.

"What's wrong with letting me dress you in an acceptable way?"

He expected to see her smile. Thought perhaps this conversation was just some of the regular teasing Cass doled out. She'd joked about his "farmer John" clothes before. But this time, her face held not a hint of mirth.

"I'm not going to dress up and make a show of things on my first meeting with them," Grayson explained. "They'll see me like this eventually, so they might as well get to know the real me from the start."

"You need to eradicate the hick from your wardrobe before stepping foot in my mom's house. That's just the way it is."

The words stung. It was code for "You're not good enough for me."

"I don't want to change," he said, his words measured. "My clothes are comfortable. But they're more than that. They're part of my identity."

"I know..." Her cheeks darkened with a blush. "Maybe it would just be better if we kept this thing, well..."

"A secret?" he blurted out. "Cass, please help me to understand what you're saying because, from where I'm standing, it sounds like you don't like what makes me, me.

Like what we do together behind closed doors is some kind of a dirty little secret. Am I good enough to bang but not good enough to meet your family?"

"You'll never be good enough to meet my family." She shrugged. "That's just the way it is. I'm fine with keeping things the way they are, but if you're not, then that's up to you."

His hackles stood, but he felt too strongly toward Cass to let what they had go so easily. He gave in. "Fine. I'll shop for some fancy clothes with you, then. Get some stuff that will satisfy your mother's... discerning taste."

She blinked in shock, like she hadn't thought he'd agree to it.

"Well?" he asked when she didn't reply.

Slowly, she shook her head as she eyed him head to toe. "It still won't work."

"You just said it would!"

"I know, but I just imagined dressing you up, and the fact of the matter is, even a new wrapper wouldn't be enough to hide your roots from my mother. Even if I polished and shined you up like a member of posh society, I could never rid you of your hick heart."

"What does that mean?" he asked through gritted teeth, trying not to lose his temper. "I've never gotten complaints about my manners." His family brought him up to be a gentleman. Sure, he'd often come in from the field without remembering to take off his boots and he'd track in some mud through the house, but did stuff like that really make him unworthy?

Did being from the country mean he had some terrible disease or blight against his character?

When she failed to answer, he knew it wasn't worth continuing. "I guess that settles it then."

Cass had trashed him hard enough that he wasn't even willing to put her in the friend zone. As far as he was concerned, he had an obligation to work with ASS, but that was it. They'd solve this case, ensure his students were safe, and go their separate ways.

The peahen blinked with long, dark lashes, taking him in. He expected a quip from her—the Cass he knew never missed a chance to cut someone with her words… or her talons—but she kept her ruby lips sealed. Instead, she perched on the corner of the table, crossing one leg over the other. Grayson's eyes were drawn to the long, beautiful legs that sprouted from her pink mini-skirt. But then he caught sight of something new: a long, dark scar running up the outside of her right ankle, cutting through her medium-brown skin. The mark was almost a foot long. He flicked his eyes back up to Cass' face as she rummaged through her giant purse. He hoped she didn't see his eyes linger on the gnarled line streaking up her leg.

He'd heard a rumor she was out of action for quite some time but never learned the details. ASS didn't like to share information with FUC unless it was completely necessary, and he could understand that an agency would want to keep the personal business of an agent secret.

Yet, now he wondered if the scar was a part of the reason why she was off active duty for so long. *It's not my concern,* he reminded himself. Not that he didn't care. He was glad she was all right, but the less he knew about Cass the better. She'd made it very clear years ago that he was well below her dress code. An inappropriate mate. What had he been thinking anyway? A hound and a peafowl? How ridiculous.

Cass pulled a black tube of what he presumed to be lipstick from her purse. He was about to make a snide remark when she pulled off the bottom secret-agent-style. She slid out a hidden flash drive. "Here's the files you requested on the red-tailed hawk," she explained, her voice smooth as satin. "I would have given it to you last night in your office, but you seemed keen on getting rid of me quickly."

The bird of prey in question had attempted to kidnap one of Grayson's students, Ellie Talbot, last year. After Ellie had recovered in the rehab wing after being experimented on, she decided to enroll in FUCN'A. The poor kid was temporarily recaptured by the hawk during her first assignment off campus. What terrible luck. Grayson wanted to deep-fry the bird responsible since Ellie was on the assignment for his class. Grayson had hoped that ASS would shake their tailfeathers and hustle after the intel on the rogue raptor. Instead, it took cutting through a mile of red tape for the agency to *start* the process of tracking down their foe. He should've expected that. ASS was a bunch of asses. Aside from his brief roll in the hay with Agent Sparks years ago, he couldn't say that he got along with any of their on-loan agents. As far as he was concerned, they were a bunch of bird-brained bastards afraid to ruffle their feathers and get down to business.

His mouth hung open in surprise when Cass got right to the point. That was unlike the avian shifter from a decade ago. That Cass never missed a chance to strut around for a bit, forcing others to wait until she felt good and ready to disclose what she knew. Instead of the banter he'd expected, he got the information he requested. It was later than expected, but at least he received it.

"Are we waiting for others to attend the meeting?" she asked, snapping him back to the moment.

"No, it's just us. FUC hasn't yet deigned to send other agents to work on this case. They consider our target a low-level lackey and not a considerable threat." He shook his head. He understood there were bigger cases, madder scientists, but a threat this close to the Academy should warrant more attention, in his opinion.

"We could have met in your office instead of taking up a whole room for just the two of us," she replied, sliding off the table and into a chair while he popped the drive into his laptop.

"Meeting rooms are for mission briefs," he muttered, opening the files and projecting them to the big screen. What he left unsaid was that it had felt much too intimate to have her in his personal space. His office was his den, his safety, and he hadn't liked her scent in there, intermingling with his.

"I'm sorry there isn't more there," Cass said as Grayson clicked through the files. "Your hawk is known to ASS as a simple lackey, in it solely for the money, working for the highest bidder."

Grayson's heart sank. Typical Cass, showing up with all the pomp and circumstance, with nothing solid to present with it. All fluff. "You really came all this way to deliver me nothing?"

"No." Cass let out a sigh. "I know this on its own isn't much help, but no, I didn't come all this way to deliver nothing. I came here to help you track him down." Despite the tone Grayson used with her, Cass' voice remained soft as silk. It tickled at his senses and jiggled lose a memory of Cass nibbling on his earlobe, whispering about all the dirty things she would do to him...

A snap of her fingers brought him back to the room, where she stared at him with large hazel eyes. That's when Grayson noticed a new scar, one that cut through her left eyebrow. Another remnant from the incident that caused the jagged line down her ankle?

Cass waved her hands as if flagging down a jet. "Earth to Grayson. You home?" Annoyance had started to creep onto her face as she narrowed her eyes to slits. She shifted her round bottom in her chair, a bird about to take flight—and probably peck his eyes out for being rude.

"Yeah," he said, realizing with embarrassment how ignorant he'd just been. The hot prickle of a blush crept up his neck before settling in his cheeks. While Cass wasn't necessarily a friend, he didn't want to make her uncomfortable. He wasn't sure if it was rude to ask about the scars so pretended he noticed nothing. "I was trying to remember what Ellie told us about the hawk." His deep voice sounded hollow, like the soul had been sucked out of it. He didn't like lying. He didn't need to try to remember what Ellie had told him: he'd been thinking of this mission constantly and hadn't let a single detail go unexamined any day since he'd recovered the cadets.

Cass raised a perfectly groomed brow. "That's all in there, too." Each word dripped out of her mouth, marinated in a confused tone. She cocked her head sideways, scarlet ringlets bouncing with the quick movement. There was no doubt in Grayson's mind she'd noticed how odd he was acting. Grayson swallowed the sting of shame rising in his chest. He was acting like a complete ass and digging the hole he was standing in deeper.

"Right," he said with a drawl, stretching the word to buy time to create a legitimate excuse. Here he was, looking like the crazy one in the duo, when that was supposed to be Cass' role. *She* was known as the firecracker. The wildcard. "I was trying to remember details left out of the report." He shifted his eyes around the room, trying to hide his discomfort, too afraid to look at Cass. With her sharp eyes, she'd see right through him.

"You mean because of FUC's shoddy job at completing paperwork correctly?" she snapped.

He should have been offended by the jab, but he set himself up for it. "I mean because not every detail can be put into a report, no matter how thorough. Scents, for example." Grayson wished the brainiacs in their IT departments could find a way to store aromas. Once his Basset Hound scented something, he could track it. While the flash drive contained the last known associates, recent sightings, and even some pictures of the foul fowl, Grayson felt that knowing what it *smelled* like would be invaluable to agents like him with a well-developed olfactory sense. Especially shifters well-suited to tracking or hunting.

"I'm glad you guys stepped up the quality control." There wasn't even a hint of sarcasm in her voice. Grayson was taken aback by the positivity directed at FUC. That was very un-Cass-like.

Her watchful eyes studied him for a moment before she glanced back to the projected image. He'd closed the files, and it now featured his desktop, a picture of a sunset Grayson took while on vacation in the mountains. She smiled softly at it, and his heart prickled, pleased to see a piece of the old Cass again. As a young agent, she'd been passionate about her job, maybe a little birdbrained at times, but she'd always been competent, and together they'd always been able to track down their mark and make their arrest. Despite the mysterious scars, Cass really seemed like her old self, without as much spite, though he had occasionally loved to witness Cass cutting people to shreds in a mere sentence.

Grayson felt some of those old, warm feelings creeping back in as he thought about another place where Cass' fiery passion took center stage: in the bedroom. He cleared his throat, pushing the images back down. "Where do *you* think we should start?" She was an ASS agent after all, and their specialty was shifters with feathers. Wasn't she the expert with all the great ideas?

"There's a bird bar in the next town over, not far from here."

"Bird bar?" He wasn't familiar with such a thing. Large quantities of birds had made him nervous since childhood, when his family had a mean rooster on their farm. One day, the cock and the hens cornered Grayson. He still had a small scar on his leg from when the birds' talons dug in. To this day, the thought of flocks of avian shifters in a small area left him feeling like he'd be walking into a crowded chicken coop. He'd be up to his eyeballs in plumage.

If this was any other avian case, he would have passed. But the hawk had picked the wrong cat to go after. He'd suck it up for Ellie, his former student. He probably felt more responsible for the attack than usual since Ellie was on an assignment for his class when the bird of prey struck.

"Yeah. Birds of a feather flock together and all that." She rolled her hazel eyes. "Someone there probably has good intel or, at the very least, has seen something." As if bored, Cass pulled out her compact mirror from her large purse and fixed some of the spiral curls lining her face.

"If that's the case, then why wasn't this already mentioned to us?" He wasn't just pissed at ASS for withholding the information. There were plenty of birds working at FUCN'A, and any of them could have offered him this tidbit of information. Unfortunately, thanks to bureaucracy and mission chain of command, none of them even knew he needed that intel.

"Because your official request only wanted to know what was in our *existing* files." Her words were clipped, agitated even. "Which means that's all we were allowed to offer until we had ASS on the ground, fully part of the mission. Remember, this is essentially your fault since *your* agency made these rules." Cass absently polished the rhinestone in her pinky nail.

Not exactly true, but she had a point. "Okay. Bird

bar it is," Grayson agreed, hoping he wouldn't regret this decision. Especially if Cass insisted on driving. Which she *always* did.

3

───────

Grayson nearly kissed the asphalt of the parking lot after they arrived at the bird bar. He'd forgotten what it felt like to ride as Cass' passenger. He'd always suspected that the high heels made her press the pedals too hard, but she'd never admit to it. Either way, his stomach was more than pleased to exit to safety.

You'd think she was a cheetah shifter the way she drives—fast and weaving around any traffic in her way!

It was a miracle they didn't attempt to kill each other during the car ride. When he complained about her speed, Cass made it known what she thought of his driving, chirping about his inability to expedite their commute *"If you were a better driver, we wouldn't always take my car. You lollygag."* He didn't share her feelings.

Unfortunately, his uneasiness didn't dissipate

with leaving the car. The bird bar loomed before them. Childhood rooster incident aside, Grayson had trouble trusting animals he couldn't easily track. Or ones that could swoop him up and carry him away, like what had happened to Ellie last year. And now they were hunting down the bird of prey that could do just that. He didn't like it. Any of it. And birds just *smelled* funny.

All except Cass, his inner hound reminded him.

Shake it off, he retorted. The fear caused by her speed had managed to distract him away from being in such close proximity to her, but her scent lingered and kept tempting old memories to surface. *Focus.*

His nose wrinkled as they entered the establishment. Cass inspected him, noting his expression. "Relax. They're not going to peck your eyes out inside the bar." A sly smile spread across her face.

Grayson narrowed his eyes, his brain filling with scenes from horror movies using birds as a means for the demise of a character. Until Cass said it, he hadn't thought of that scenario. He pulled a pair of sunglasses out of his jacket pocket and put them on. He'd rather be safe than sorry.

Cass shook her head, curls bouncing. "You look ridiculous."

He wanted to snap back a quip about how they were entering a dive bar and she was dressed to the nines but held his tongue. Right now, Grayson wanted to avoid her opening her bird beak and calling attention to them.

He followed Cass through the door and into the dark room. The dim light of the interior was enough to catch the rhinestones on her heels. They sparkled with the motion of her gait but didn't distract from the smell of sweat and feathers tickling his nose. Grayson struggled to hold in a sneeze.

Despite not wanting to call attention toward themselves, their entrance was definitely noticed. All the patrons stopped what they were doing like they were in a Western movie and a group of outsiders had just entered the establishment. Grayson even thought he saw a man spit on the floor out of the corner of his eye. Gross.

Unfazed, Cass continued to walk up to the wooden bar, heels clacking on the cracked linoleum floor—intentionally, Grayson knew, since she could very well walk silently when she wanted to.

All eyes followed her, assessing her every move. Grayson stayed on edge, ready for anything. He'd never felt more unwelcome in his life.

Not counting what Cass said back to him in Toronto, of course.

I should have worn a different pair of heels. Cass sauntered up to the bar, cringing as her shoes stuck to the floor from whatever substances had been spilled here and there. If a wad of gum ended up on her sole, she would flip. Feathers would fly. She had a pair of field heels for this reason, but no, she had to wear her lucky pair today.

She hesitated before setting her purse on the wet bar top, inspecting the grime staining the wood. Instead, she balanced it on the crook of her arm before pulling out some cash. She wasn't about to trash her favorite handbag, too.

The bartender glanced up from the sink where she was wiping down a pint glass. "We don't serve your kind here," she said with a rough whiskey voice.

"Peafowl?" Cass asked innocently. The corners of her lips raised in a mischievous grin.

"No. Mutts." The bartender crossed her arms across her chest.

Cass smelled Grayson's anger rising. He'd tensed up the moment they'd entered the bar, and she hadn't been sure if it was the quality of the bar he didn't like or the fact that it was filled with bird shifters.

She glanced back at her companion and did her best to give him a reassuring wink, urging him to keep his cool. Cass turned back to the wall of booze in front of her, tapping the bills in her hand on the wooden counter. "He's not drinking, so it shouldn't be a problem."

Grayson cleared his throat, probably struggling with not reminding Cass that she shouldn't be drinking on the job. He always was a stickler for the rules. Most canine shifters seemed to be that way. Easily trained and forever obedient.

"Fine." The bartender set down the glass she was drying and reached for the money Cass had set down —more than enough for a drink. She counted it and nodded, clearly accepting the large tip with the understanding that she'd need to offer some information in return.

"Can I have a Cosmo?" Cass asked with a sweet smile. What bird didn't enjoy a good cocktail?

The bartender nodded, though the corners of her mouth seemed condemned by gravity to remain turned down. It was the best RBF—Resting Bitch Face—Cass'd seen in a while. Impressive. Cass wondered what bird species she might be. With a face like that, perhaps pied starling. There was really no way for her to know, though. She didn't have a great sense of scent to begin with, and it was hard to scent the differences in bird species. It wasn't like figuring out if a mammal was a lion or tiger or hound.

As the bartender flittered off to make the concoction, the rest of the bar went back about its business. The jukebox started up with all the conversations. Soon all the patrons chirped as usual.

As soon as the drink was placed in front of her, Cass decided to start her line of questioning. "We're looking for a hawk that makes a habit of flying away with shifters in its talons. You hear anything about this?"

The bartender leaned in on her elbows. Cass mirrored her, closing the gap between them. The woman pointed to a group in black leather vests in the far corner of the bar. "Do you see that biker gang?" she asked. Cass nodded. "They had a member go missing last week. Might be a good place to start."

Cass thanked her and plucked up her martini glass, surprised this establishment had fancy glassware. She expected to get her drink in a plastic cup. *This dump has class*, she thought, crossing the crowded room with Grayson following a few steps behind. She cursed under her breath after stepping on another sticky tile. These shoes were definitely either getting burned or would need some TLC to clean the gunk off of them.

Five gang members, three male and two female, chugged down the remains of their longnecks before picking up new bottles of beer in front of them. One of the larger males had his back to them. "Murderous Crows" was stitched into the back of his black, faux-leather vest. A layer of fat coated his large, muscular biceps, but Cass assumed he could still pack a punch if threatened. She had no intention of testing her theory.

Someone at the table gestured for the large man to turn around. Cass took in his long beard and the scar across the bridge of his crooked nose. "What do you want?" he asked, his voice gruff and loud, making it clear they weren't going to be easy to talk to.

"I heard one of your gang went missing. We want to help," Cass offered, trying to keep her tone neutral. She flashed her ASS badge, wanting to be upfront about her status as law enforcement before starting the conversation. Better for them to know the facts right away and not accuse them of subterfuge later. Now, to convince him that they were on their side. Otherwise, she couldn't earn their trust and they'd clamp their beaks so tight a caw couldn't escape.

"Why do you care?" a woman with frizzy bleach-blonde hair piped up. She narrowed her eyes at them.

"Could be your missing friend fell foul of a red-tailed hawk we're looking for," Grayson explained, startling Cass. He'd been so quiet so far she'd almost wondered if he'd snuck out the door when she wasn't looking.

The large male tilted back his head as he took a long swig of beer from the brown bottle in his hand. He inspected Cass and Grayson, narrowing his eyes. "Who are you two? The misfit police? One of you looks like you just stepped off the farm and the other looks like you're about to judge a beauty pageant." The whole gang of crows burst out in cackling laughter.

Once upon a time, she would have been pegged as a contestant, not a judge, but that fact didn't ruffle her. "Just because I am fashionable doesn't mean I don't know how to kick ass," Cass retorted. "Don't underestimate the amount of damage I could do with these stilettos. They're great for stabbing." Okay, maybe she'd never stab anyone with her favorite pair of heels. One of her field ones… absolutely. Even one of her out-of-season ones, sure. If she was in a jam and a shoe needed to be sacrificed, then so be it. But her lucky pair? That would only happen if things turned life or death. Even so, these crows didn't need to know that.

"For the record," Grayson butted in, showing his badge as Cass had already done, "we're FUC and ASS."

"You're fucking ass?" the blonde lady asked, raising an eyebrow in confusion. "I hardly know you. Why do I care what you two do in your spare time?"

Cass shook her head. These stupid acronyms left everyone confused. "I'm with ASS, he's from FUC," she corrected. "As in, agents."

The group still looked confused, some cocking their heads to the side, others wrinkling their bows. After scratching their heads, they seemed ready to let it slide and move on.

"What about the hawk?" an older man in the back piped up. He rubbed the greying scruff on his jawline.

"A red-tailed hawk shifter tried to kidnap one of my FUCN'A cadets," Grayson explained. "We think the hawk is a gun for hire, working for scientists who experiment on shifters." He was unable to hide the disdain in his voice. Cass knew him well enough to deduce how important his students were to him. It was clear his FUCN'A job as an instructor was more than a paycheck. He cared for his pupils. Cass' heart skipped a beat when she noticed the worry spread across his face as his brows rumpled in concern. Grayson always had a big heart, and she was glad to see that years at this job hadn't dampened that. It was so easy to become burned out and calloused.

The older biker adjusted the black bandanna covering his balding head. His face scrunched up as he thought, deepening his wrinkles. "Joe did mention a hawk he met. Said she used to hang out with a flock of seagulls in the park downtown."

"You're right!" the blonde chick piped up, nearly springing out of her chair with excitement. "I think her name was Cindy... or Sandy. Joe's been struggling to find a girl since he and his ol' lady broke up."

"Was she a red-tail?" Cass asked, glad they could offer her some information. It was more than they had before they walked in.

The burly man answered, "She was definitely a hawk, but I don't know what variety."

"When did Joe go missing?"

"Last week, Sunday." The burly crow shifter leaned back in his chair, crossing his arms. "Yeah, now that I think about it... Joe said his new friend had 'something special planned' for him or something."

"It was something special, all right," the blonde agreed. "We haven't seen him since."

"We drink here every night," the older crow explained with a shrug. "We suspected something happened to Joe when he stopped showing, but what could we do about it? The law ain't going to care about a dude from a biker gang going missing."

"Well, then I'm glad we came in here," Cass said, placing her card on their table and then setting her Cosmo down on the corner of it. "Thank you for the information. Hopefully we'll find some trace of your friend."

The group looked offended by the drink, but one of them scooped up the card.

"Now what?" Grayson asked with a sigh of relief when they exited the bar. "Go to the park and track down the flock of seagulls?"

"If not the hawk herself." Cass nodded.

Mentally crossing her fingers, she led Grayson toward her car.

4

Grayson's stomach lurched as Cass hammered the gas after the light turned green. He thought her highway driving was bad enough, but downtown driving was even worse, at least when it came to cursing about all the other drivers and pedestrians along the way. She seemed to have the biggest case of road rage he had ever seen when she rolled down her window to scream at a bunch of cyclists, "There's bike paths for a reason!"

Grayson slid down in his seat out of embarrassment when she gave them the finger. Was it a peacock thing or just a Cass thing to drive so aggressively? And more importantly, how could he convince her to let him drive next time? He didn't think he could handle another day of her chauffeuring him around. As a dog shifter, he usually enjoyed car rides, but that was not the case with Cass behind the wheel.

He was beyond pleased when she finally pulled into the park, swinging into a parallel parking space flawlessly.

"How do you think we'll recognize these gulls?" she asked, stepping out of the bright red car. The rhinestones in the frame of her large sunglasses sparkled in the warm light of the early evening sun.

"I can sniff out birds but can't discern the species," Grayson answered, pulling his eyes away from Cass to scan the vast park. A few couples watched their children play on the swings. Lone joggers traversed the paved pathway that meandered through the sparse trees and neatly mowed grass. These shifters could be anyone.

Letting his nose guide him, he settled on a small group of people gathered around an overflowing garbage can. Some of them circled the trash receptacle, bobbing their heads as they walked, squawking and shoving at each other if one got too close. Nearby, a man perched on a picnic table eating French fries out of a carboard container while another male tried to steal some when he wasn't looking.

"I have a feeling that may be them." Grayson shook his head, disbelieving they were about to question such a foolish group of gulls. Dealing with a gang of crows was one thing, but seagulls in the park? The sooner they found the evil hawk, the sooner he'd never have to deal with another bird-brained group again—thank goodness. While it was true some hounds were known for hunting birds, it wasn't his thing. His senses preferred game that traveled on the ground.

Cass lifted her glasses to get a better look. She wrinkled up her nose in disgust and then nodded. It seemed even bird shifters weren't too fond of certain groups. She looked back toward Grayson and extended her hand as if to say, "after you."

He didn't move right away. Instead of obeying, he assessed her behavior. It was so unlike the Cass he'd once known to not make some sort of sarcastic comment. Maybe compare dirty, lazy dogs like Grayson to the garbage-loving seagulls. Come to think of it, she'd not made a comment about his clothing at all since she'd arrived.

He'd never gone a day knowing her without hearing some sort of "suggestion" regarding his fashion choices. Clearly, based on how she was dressed, fashion was still an interest of hers, but something was different—aside from the scars he'd noticed. There was something else changed about her.

Cass cocked her head to the side, taking in his pensive expression. "I know hounds have a one-track mind and all, but what's on yours today?"

He was thrown off by the question, which,

despite the word choice, lacked any hint of innuendo. No, the way she peered at him came off as more intimate. Not the usual surface-level Cass. He tried to crack a friendly smile, but his face didn't cooperate. He was too stuck on figuring out what he was missing about her. "You just seem different," he admitted. His deep voice softened at the words, as if afraid to utter them.

She crossed her arms and leaned up against her shiny car. A shy smile lifted up the corners of her ruby lips. "I am."

He wanted to ask more, probe about her scars and her time out of the field, but before he could construct the right question, Cass said, "We need to interrogate them before they fly the coop."

She nodded toward the possible gang of seagulls. There wasn't a sure way to spot a specific bird type, but if Grayson was a betting man, he'd put his money on them.

He nodded at her logic and headed into the park. He'd have to figure out how Cass had changed later. Right now, he had a bird to track.

Cass' chest swelled with pride at Grayson's words. Though it wasn't the time or the place to start such a discussion, it lifted her spirits that Grayson had an open mind about her. They'd been together for less than a whole day and he'd noticed she was different. This was more than she'd hoped for.

She was intent to prove that, while her feathers hadn't changed, the mental scars had led to traumatic growth. Like a butterfly shedding its cocoon, Cass was a new woman. She would no longer look down on others like her mother had trained her to. The value of people was not measured by appearances. Her mother had bemoaned this fact when Cass lay in her hospital bed and never let up on her opinion until Cass was walking on her own and covering her scars with makeup. That's when Cass realized that, while her mother dressed like a celebrity, she was rotten on the inside. A fate Cass dodged a bullet on.

She could've easily walked in her mother's foot-steps. Instead, she learned a life lesson and chose to be different, to free herself of that judgmental mentality. It took effort to not fall back to scruti-nizing others all the time. All that criticism and hatred weighed her mother down. Cass wouldn't be that. It had taken a car crash to open her eyes. Not at first, but after some time.

She regretted she couldn't have had that epiphany when she'd first met Grayson. The hound dog's first trip to the big city, with a peahen as his tour guide while they worked a joint ASS-FUC mission. She'd taken him to the hotspots and dive bars with the tastiest food, and while she did, she learned what a real gentleman was like. Grayson held open doors for her, waited for her to order first, listened while she blathered on about any topic, and offered her his coat when the nights turned chilly.

As they worked more cases together and became closer, he told her his dreams. Welcomed her like family. Shown her love that she'd never thought possible and cared for her in a way she'd never been in her whole life. He'd never criticized what she wore or how she styled her hair, as her mother had. He enjoyed her quick wit and strong personality.

For a short time, she'd lived on cloud nine.

An excited phone call home to Mother changed all that. She'd expected Mother to be hung up on his being a hound shifter since Mother had always hoped she'd find her way into a peacock's harem. Be taken in by someone fancy from a high-class family.

Cass tried to explain to her mother that Grayson was sweet and caring, coming from a warm, supportive family. That he was the kind of man one could only dream of. That hadn't mattered. Mother took one look at the picture Cass sent via text and coldly chirped, *"Get rid of him before he tarnishes our name."*

"I know he looks like he's fresh off the farm, but he has impeccable hygiene," Cass tried to explain, to no avail. Her mother wouldn't hear of it, and Cass was crushed. For once she wanted Mother to accept her independence. Just one time she wanted to be with who she wanted, not whom Mother chose. Mother

had run Cass' entire life like a drill sergeant, telling her what to wear and who to be friends with, setting her up on dates, even picking out her university. Cass shuddered at the memory of how much control she'd allowed her mother to have. And instead of growing a spine and letting her true feathers show, she bowed down to the woman's wishes. Again.

But not anymore.

Cass followed Grayson to the group surrounding the trash, their inane chatter already drifting to her ears. Seagull shifters talked too much. But then again, a lot of avian shifters did. Heck, even she found it difficult to keep her beak closed sometimes. Not that all bird shifters shared this trait. Her best friend, Bianca, was a songbird shifter. While she enjoyed singing, she wasn't as chatty as other birds.

The gull group stopped circling the metal can of garbage as Cass and Grayson neared. They looked at them expectantly, though she couldn't tell if they would be more likely to attack or flee if provoked.

"Do any of you know a biker by the name of Joe?" Grayson asked, stopping a few feet away. He lifted his nose in a way she knew to mean he was scenting the air. Probably double-checking that this group was shifters. They had to be careful. If this was a group of humans, they couldn't let it slip that shifters existed.

"Joe?" the man eating the fries asked, turning his head to stare at them from the side with one eye. A chorus of "Joe" erupted as the rest of the group echoed the name. The second man at the table chose not to join and instead snuck a few fries while the other was distracted.

Cass took a step back. While it was true that shifters took on some of the characteristics of their animal, these gulls seemed to be over-identifying with their bird.

"Yes. Joe." Grayson adjusted his sunglasses and shifted uncomfortably but didn't back down. "He was supposed to come here last week to meet someone named Cindy or Sandy. Sound familiar?"

Now they erupted into a mixture of "Joe," "Cindy," and "Sandy." Cass became more unsettled. *Something's not right here.* They weren't like any flock of birds Cass had ever been around—and as an ASS agent, she'd been around many. Instead, they seemed unnatural, like an experiment gone wrong. Were they mixed with parrots? So far, the group didn't seem able to form their own words or phrases, only repeat what Grayson said.

Grayson turned to Cass. "Do you speak gull?"

"No." She bit her lip. "Gray, I think there's something wrong with them."

They picked up on the word "wrong" and began echoing it.

"Really?" Grayson raised a brow. "I guess I'll take your word for it."

"I mean it. This isn't normal behavior, even for bird shifters." Cass hadn't seen anything like it. She took another step back, horrified by what she witnessed. Who would do something like this to the gull shifters?

The five shifters circling the trash started flapping their arms and squawking. The man with the fries snapped at the other man on the table with his teeth after noticing him steal another fry.

"At least they can't peck your eyes out," Cass tried to reassure Grayson. She could tell under the sunglasses that his eyes were wide. He was well beyond his comfort zone with this case.

Humans in the park stopped to record the scene with their cellphone cameras. This wasn't good. The shifting community tried hard to keep their supernatural abilities secret from regular people. If shit got out of hand and this group changed into a flock of seagulls, they'd have to grab a COOCHI—Corrective Outdoor-shift Or Calming of Humans Incident — form. It would assist both FUC and ASS in following the status of the coverup of the public shift. Excuses could range from gas leaks causing hallucinations to PR stunts for the local zoo. Cass' brain raced with excuses to explain away this train wreck.

She turned to Grayson and said loud enough for the gathering crowd to hear, "The artists call this 'Angry Seagulls.' It's a protest against littering."

Grayson nodded, saying nothing. That seemed to satisfy some of the gathering people, who, after clapping, dispersed back into the park. A few remained behind until they realized the "performers" weren't going to do much more than flap their arms and pace while repeating various words and names. Their faces hinted at their boredom before they meandered back along the path away from the gulls.

Cass was at a loss. In all her years of an agent, she hadn't been in a situation like this. It would be one thing to occur where no one could see, but in public? This wasn't good at all.

Do you speak gull? Grayson's earlier question reverberated through her mind. "I do!" she exclaimed, turning to him. He raised a curious eyebrow. "Speak gull, that is. Birds can communicate with each other... in a manner of speaking." Birds were able to recognize the general meaning of some calls from other species. If she could find a place to shift... She glanced around, looking for a restroom. With any luck, she'd find one cleaner than the bar they were just in, or she would have to replace more pieces of her wardrobe. Though, the more she thought about it, the more fun a shopping trip sounded.

The human-shaped gulls squawked louder, some of them mere rasps since their vocal cords struggled to make the sound. A few hopped excitedly.

"Are you talking about shifting?" Grayson whispered. "How am I going to explain away a peacock the size of an ostrich?"

"For one, I'm a peahen," she corrected, puffing out

her chest with pride. "And just make up some crap about me in costume, protesting the dangers of growth hormones in our food or some shit."

She waved her hand in a flourish. Her nails glistened in the light of the fading sun, dipping below the line of trees at the distant end of the park. She pointed a finger at the screeching group. "Keep them here and happy until I get back."

Without further instruction, she padded off to the nearest bathroom.

5

This is horse shit. Grayson grew up on a farm around animals and shifters alike, and he'd never been more uneasy in his life. And Cass had left him. Alone. With these crazy bird-brained people. He grimaced as one rooted through the trash littering the ground, pecking at wrappers with his pointed nose. As a young pup, Grayson may have liked knocking over the kitchen trash and spreading refuse around during temper tantrums, but it was something he'd grown out of.

Speaking of growing and changing, he couldn't help but think about Cass... and himself. Cass was the same, yet different than the woman he'd met years ago, but him? He'd been so naïve back then. Becoming a FUC agent was the first time he'd met shifters outside of the canine community where he grew up. He'd never considered the various cultural differences of animal societies until he met other agents, and most of those in FUC were mammals. Sure, there were rare exceptions, like Jessie Cygnclair and Clarice Tertius, but he'd never gotten to know them very well.

Which meant he was in for culture shock when he met Cass from ASS. A beautiful peafowl who made his heart race from the first time he met her hazel eyes. The perfect balance of green and brown, reminding him of the rich forests back home that surrounded his family farm. Her gaze made him feel just that—at home.

She dressed to the nines, yet she wasn't stuck up, as he'd heard many other ASS could be. Cass gave him a chance, really talked to him. Opened up. He got to learn about her and her family, but he thought she was joking when she explained she was expected to join a peacock's harem—until he realized she was serious.

So Grayson decided to drop the judgments and learn. He educated himself on traditional and non-traditional shifter households. And human ones, too. It opened up his eyes to new cultures and societies. While he discovered many differences, he enjoyed learning about similarities. At the heart of everything was family. And love.

Cass had disclosed she wanted a non-traditional family for a peafowl. She felt that being one of many peahens in a harem with one peacock wouldn't float her boat.

"I don't get along well with peacocks," she explained one night while they drank champagne and soaked in the hot tub of their hotel suite. "I enjoy attention. I don't need a peacock trying to outshine me. And I want my man all to myself."

She spoke of many regrets of her childhood and the tumultuous relationship with her mother. Being one of many chicks in her father's harem didn't suit her either. Nor her mother. According to Cass, when she was six, her mother took her and flew the coop to venture out on their own. Unfortunately, even though her mother had fled that lifestyle, she still somehow expected Cass to return to it.

Back then, he'd thought he and Cass were close. When they'd met, he felt accepted by her. A city woman who didn't mind the dirt on his boots. Then, something changed. Out of nowhere, she turned cold. More critical of his clothes, particularly the boots. Since he'd not dressed any differently than he had when they'd met, he thought her attitude might be because he'd done something wrong. It kept him up many nights, but he couldn't find one misstep he took with Cass. Then, one morning when he got back to their hotel room after picking up coffee, she cut him deep with her words. It wasn't just a one-off comment about his "farmer John" clothes but a full-on insult to him, his family, and his home community.

He'd wanted to leave immediately with his tail between his legs in defeat, yet he decided to stick it out. Finish their mission. Catch the bad guy. And they did. Then, they went their separate ways.

Until days ago, when Grayson learned who the on-loan ASS agent was who'd be assisting him.

"Sooo…" He rocked back on the heels of his boots as the seagull gang tired of their trash and started to look curiously in his direction. Cass said to keep them calm. What the hell could he possibly say that would do that? Grayson watched the man perched on the end of the picnic table stare at the one with the container of food. "Hit up any good fast-food restaurants lately?"

They all stopped what they were doing and cocked their heads sideways, staring at Grayson with one eye before they started walking toward him. Their heads jerked with each step as they lurched closer. Grayson moved back a foot and adjusted his sunglasses. It was getting harder to see in them as the sun set, but he'd prefer to leave the park with both eyes.

Wishing he had a pocket full of worms, he shuffled back farther and bumped into something large.

He whirled around to find the grey beak of a giant peahen. Cass wriggled the plume of the crest of bare-shafted feathers atop her head. She held her head high and proud, and Grayson stepped aside so she could do her thing. Her long neck bobbed with each step, and he watched the coloring of her feathers fluctuate from dark grey to a soft, metallic blue with the motion. She wasn't as colorful as a peacock but was just as beautiful.

The flock of human gulls eyed her up. A few regular people stopped to gawk at the scene. "It's an animal rights protest," Grayson grunted. The display raised a few eyebrows, but after his explanation, they left satisfied. They were lucky it was so close to sunset and the park was emptying. He'd hate to have to continue to make up excuses to a larger crowd.

Cass trilled at the confused shifters, and to Grayson's relief, their shrieking slowed. It worked. They stopped surging toward him while their eyes remained plastered on Cass and her fluffy plumage instead of him.

With their attention fully captured, he took the opportunity to take out his phone and call for backup. FUCN'A would need to send any agents they had to help collect these weirdos. At least they'd get some help since FUCN'A wasn't just for shifters to train to be FUC agents; it also doubled as a hospital and recovery center for experiments trying to find their place in the world. His former student Ellie—the one who was temporarily abducted last year by the hawk they were keen to catch—lived in the hospital wing for a while as she recovered from being experimented on and before she decided to train to become a FUC agent. It was during her training that the hawk tried to capture her, likely to examine her interesting abilities—Ellie could bend light around herself to appear invisible. Resourceful Ellie was able to escape before Sandy could bring her back to the doctor who employed her.

He bypassed admin and dialed in directly to Alyce Cooper, black llama shifter and director of FUCN'A.

"We're going to need a rescue team and more FUC agents at the park downtown," he quickly informed her the moment she answered. He briefly described the incident and the behavior he and Cass had witnessed. He assured her that Cass had managed to herd them all together for the moment.

"I'll have a team there immediately with a medical transport."

"Thanks."

After putting his phone back in his jeans pocket, he looked back toward the group of seagull-shifters who thought they were birds.

Wait... Where's Cass? The giant peahen was nowhere to be seen. Cass was missing!

One minute Cass was warbling to a group of gulls, and the next, a black bag was put over her and she was being carried off. Bird-napped, and Grayson missed the whole thing. He was too busy barking off orders to FUC.

Struggling to free herself got her nowhere, and before she knew it, she'd been tossed like a sack of garbage, landing hard in an echoey chamber. An engine starting was quickly followed by movement as the vehicle started off. Then, the bag was removed from her, and she saw the empty van around her.

Empty other than the two kidnappers in there with her.

"Hurry, tie her up!" the driver shouted to the man in the back with her.

She snapped at him, but he was ready for it and managed to loop lengths of rope around her and successfully pinned down her wings. She could have pecked him, but she didn't want to risk him deciding to break her neck. Since he didn't think to tie her legs, she had half a mind to shred him with her powerful talons but decided it may be more fruitful to see where they were taking her. If the two that nabbed her were related to their hawk case, any information would be invaluable.

She hunkered down, nestling her breast into the floor of the van. She might as well be comfortable while she thought out a plan. When they arrived at the destination, Cass could probably get out of the rope they'd wound around her wings if she shifted, but then she'd be naked too. She just hoped Gray picked up her belongings from the bathroom before leaving the park. Not only would she like to have some covering to shift back into human form but her favorite purse and heels were there. A mournful cry trilled out her beak.

"Quiet back there!" one of the captors snarled. Apparently, they didn't know how upsetting it was to lose a designer handbag and rhinestone stilettos. Whoever they were, Cass was sure they had bad taste.

The wheels beneath her bounded along poorly paved streets, drawing her attention to the fact that she hated anyone else driving. She'd always preferred to be the one behind the wheel, but after her accident, it had intensified. She wanted the control of driving and hated to hand it off to others. She also still loved to drive fast—too fast, if Grayson were to be listened to—but that had been something she'd had to work on. When she first drove after her accident, she'd been nervous. She fought through it, though, because she wasn't going to allow them to take away her need for speed. That had always been a part of her because, when she first learned to drive, her fancy footwear had made her press the gas pedal a bit too close to the floor, and that's just how she became accustomed to driving.

As far as the road rage Grayson accused her of? Yeah… She might be a little testier behind the wheel, as she stayed on alert for any potential accidents. People drove distracted and didn't pay attention, and she had absolutely no patience for that anymore. If she honked at them, they deserved it. *Put your fucking phone down and focus on driving!* And the cyclist on the road instead of the bike path? Were they *asking* to be hurt by those distracted drivers?

She squawked as the driver took a turn too sharply, and he hollered at her to shut it again.

"What do you think she'll do to this one?" the other assailant asked, his voice a low growl.

Is the "she" the red-tailed hawk we've been chasing? Cass took stock of the intel she had at the moment. There were three people involved in her abduction: the two men in the van and a woman, whom she assumed they were driving her to meet. Considering the way the man worded his question, she gathered this wasn't about having a conversation or getting roughed up. It was more likely this was about torture or experimentation.

If the group of gulls was any indication regarding the outcomes of said research, she was hoping for torture.

6

Ten minutes after Cass disappeared, a swarm of FUC agents buzzed about the park. One special faction tended to the seagull shifters, delicately triaging the situation and planning to transport them to the hospital wing of WANC, where they'd receive the best medical and psychological care. A second team was interacting with humans in the vicinity to see if the cover story of "protesting artists" was holding. A final team of agents was to assist Grayson in tracking down Cass and her possible abductors.

Grayson pushed aside the thought of the amount of paperwork he'd have to complete following this incident—that was the aspect of the job he dreaded most—and focused instead on searching the area for clues. He already sent an agent to collect Cass' belongings from the restroom. When they returned holding Cass' clothes, shoes, and handbag, Grayson knew she was gone. Cass would only leave her belongings in a disgusting public bathroom if it were a life-and-death situation.

"She either ran off, following a lead, or she's been taken," he concluded.

Grayson traversed the park to the restrooms, taking in the scene for anything out of place that could hint to Cass' whereabouts. Though his senses in human form were preternatural, they didn't compare to his expanded capacity when in hound form.

He'd have to put his Basset olfactory system to the test and use his nose to detect clues about her captors.

He tapped the nearest FUC agent on the shoulder. "I'm going to find a private place to shift. Please guard the entrance and bag my clothes while I sniff around."

The agent nodded, no questions asked, trailing him to the small building where he would act as a guard so no unsuspecting human would stumble in with Grayson in mid-shift. That would be awkward. And require more paperwork.

After ensuring all the toilet stalls were vacant, Grayson neatly piled his clothes on the diaper changing station. He relaxed into the transformation, like shrugging off a comfortable robe. His bones shifted and joints cracked as they rotated for him to walk better on all fours. It was a strange sensation, yet not unpleasant. The hair on his body thickened and grew, tingling the flesh around it. Fur sprouted across his body, changing color to the white coat and brown spots he sported in dog form.

Grayson padded out of the bathroom on four paws, the concrete floor cooling him down with each step. His long, velvety ears wafted scents toward his black nose. He scanned all of them, searching for Cass' trail. Soon he picked it up. Even in peahen form, she still smelled of coconut, though it was mixed with the dusty odor of feathers.

He followed the essence of Cass to where the group of bird shifters gathered near the trash cans and picnic tables. He found the spot where he'd stood earlier. Cass' sweet fragrance lingered there as well. Then it careened off down the trail. He inhaled deeply, trying to gather as much information as his snout could. Farther down the sidewalk, two other scents lingered with hers. They were a sharp contrast to Cass with their oil, grit, and woody undertones.

Where the path met the street, the trail went cold. Grayson bayed. His team of agents poured into the area with their forensic tools, scouting for clues. Grayson noted the scent of pine mixed in with the dark bouquet of dirt, left from the tires of the parked vehicle. Something else was mixed in too. Cedar maybe. He howled again. A FUC agent peeled off of the pack to scoop up traces of the material left behind. Hopefully something would lead them to Cass.

They must have been close to the truth if she was snatched. Someone didn't like them sniffing around the park. With any luck, they'd be one step closer to finding the hawk.

Grayson and the other agents scoured the area for more evidence. He knew Cass could take care of herself, but he still worried. She was his partner and responsibility. How did they grab her without him noticing? He hadn't thought he'd turned away from the group for that long while he'd spoken on his phone, and he hadn't had problems when he was left watching the gulls. Still, he shouldn't have let his guard down.

If anything happened to her, it was on no one but him.

The van pulled into a warehouse, and the black bag was put back over her head. When the driver got out, a bad stench flooded her senses. The waft of dirty chicken coop hit Cass' nostrils like a punch to the gut, and suddenly she was thankful she wasn't in human form wearing her favorite stilettos. She'd have to burn them for sure if they touched the ground anywhere near here.

She strained her round eyes, trying to see through

the sack. It was useless. Cass would have the same chance of seeing if her purse was dropped over her head. None.

To escape… or not to escape. Cass stacked the pros and cons in her mind. Should she elude them now and hide out here, trying to discover what she could? Or see who they were taking her to, up close and personal? That would risk Cass not being able to free herself from the rope—or any new form of bondage her captors planned—later.

The back doors swung open, filling the van with more smelly air. Cass wished she maintained the ability to plug her nose. She'd have to practice doing it with a foot for dire situations such as this.

"Get out!" the man with the lower voice spat out.

It now made sense why they didn't tie her feet. *I guess they don't want to carry an oversized bird.*

Cass turned her long neck, her feathers shifting and realigning with the motion. Hoping they would remove the bag if she appeared incapable of functioning with it on, she pretended to try to stand and bumped into the seat in front of her. She let out a frustrated squawk, ruffling up her plumage.

"I don't think she can see well enough to stand," the other man hypothesized.

"Then help me pull her out."

"But she's a hundred-pound turkey," the other protested.

Cass warbled, voicing her displeasure at the

insult. She was not an ugly type of bird. Clearly. She was also well over their guessed weight, but she wasn't about to correct them there.

She feigned getting up again, before tumbling into the wall. She landed in a huff of feathers. There would be no award for best actress, but she tried. If only Frick and Frack would help a girl out...

The silence stretched on before the one captor whined, "You know I have a bad back."

"You do not!"

Cass wished she'd escaped earlier. It would be less annoying than listening to them bicker like hens. She rolled her eyes, even though it wouldn't be seen. It felt better than doing nothing. If she were still human, she would have ripped them to shreds with sarcasm by now. Not being able to talk was frustrating. She often used her words as a weapon.

"Let's just take the bag off. What can she do? She's a bird."

Cass didn't like being brushed off like that. Not for being a woman, not for the way she dressed or did her makeup, and certainly not for being a peafowl. She would make sure these two never underestimated her again. She'd cut them to ribbons with her talons the first chance she got. For now, she'd settle for them taking the damn bag off her head so she could view her surroundings.

"All right. But you know Sandy doesn't like it

when we go against her orders." There was a whack. "Ow! What'cha hit me for?"

"She doesn't like you using her name."

"Who she gonna tell?"

The other man laughed. It was a cruel noise that instantly sent a cold shiver down Cass' feathered back. "You're right. Once she's done with this hen, she won't be able to say a thing." He cackled.

Sounded to Cass like this Sandy *had* done something to the seagull shifters. Cass wasn't equipped to find out what today. If she had a team listening in on a wire, maybe. But working solo. Hell no. She needed to fly the coop, and fast.

One man removed her hood. She blinked, adjusting to the bright lights. His long, tangled beard tumbled down his chest, touching the top three buttons of his flannel shirt. Crumbs were stuck in it. Cass wanted to ask for the sack back to block the view.

"Come out now. Nice and easy."

She dug her talons into the metal floor of the vehicle. They scraped out a high-pitched screech. It wasn't necessary, but it was fun. The men cringed at the sound. Cass would have smiled if her beak allowed it.

She twirled around and hopped out of the back of the van. Her feet slid in the dust that coated the floor. Rough cuts of wooden beams lay around. Sawdust was sprinkled in piles like tiny, yellow snowdrifts. All the saws that would have been in the mill were gone, like everything of value had been taken when the place closed. The warped wood was left behind like bones from an ancient carcass.

Metal cages lined the walls. Large-diameter wooden dowels pierced the chain-link. The make-shift bird enclosures were stacked on top of each other. No avian creatures nestled inside. Were they in the process of starting their operation at this loca-tion? Or were they packing up to move on to the next one?

She'd seen enough of these makeshift labs to know the horrors that went on here. Some freak with an ego decides to splice together different shifter abilities? The results were always horrendous. Many ex-experiments were left with difficulty func-tioning and the inability to shift into a fully human form. Forced to be exiled to a facility like FUCN'A for the rest of their lives, hiding from the rest of the world. She'd witnessed shifters disfigured badly. And not in the way she was after her crash. These ones ended up with horns jutting from their human faces or teeth so large they couldn't shut their mouths. It churned her stomach to think of it.

And it pissed her off to think that someone felt they had the right to do this to others.

The rope around her wings and body had loos-ened around her. She puffed up her feathers when they grabbed her, allowing her bonds to remain baggy. Cass could shake them at any time. What she was waiting for was the right moment.

But what if Frick and Frack ushered her into one of these cages? Then it was game over. She'd have to fly off into the sunset before that.

"What if she shifts?" the shorter man she'd nicknamed Frack asked. His bushy eyebrows merged into one, an expression of worry.

"She won't." Frick barked a laugh. "You don't want us to see your beautiful human body, do you?" He ran a finger over the short, soft feathers of her face.

She bit him. Hard. Her beak snapped shut like a mouse trap, and the metallic taste of blood coated her thin tongue. Cass fought the urge to let go, to spit out his nasty flavor—he was as bitter and foul on the inside as out.

He bellowed. Frack's beady eyes went wide in shock, unsure how to help his partner in crime. Frick raised a fist to hit her. Instead of accepting the blow, she released his mangled digit. Shaking loose of the rope, Cass expanded her mighty wingspan, knocking both men back. Shame on them for thinking she was a helpless bird.

As the men bumbled around, trying to keep their balance, Cass looked up. Long metal rafters spanned the building. With a running hop, she flapped her wings, taking to the air. She couldn't fly long distances, but inside a warehouse, she'd do just fine.

The beam jutted out close to the ceiling but not

too close. Cass hunkered down as she landed. The metal of the girder was just wide enough for her massive talons. She roosted quite comfortably. Frick and Frack continued to stumble. One tripped over the other and landed on his ass. Cass swallowed a chuckle.

"Screw what Sandy wants. We're going to roast you on a spit!" Frick howled, saliva flying from his mouth and smattering his shabby beard.

You have to catch me first. Cass clucked. Whether or not they could understand her dismissive tone, she didn't care. *This must be how a cat feels, stalking its prey.*

Peafowl were naturally omnivorous, meaning they ate meat, insects, and plants, but Cass didn't play with her food. Eating other shifters was murder, and she wasn't about to make an exception, even if one of the men below shifted into a tasty critter, like a snake, which was on her usual bird menu.

They didn't seem able to formulate a new plan of capture. Frack squinted up at the rafters but seemed unable to find her above one of the large LED floodlights.

"Get a ladder!" Frick cried.

"We don't have any."

They didn't seem familiar with flying birds, making her wonder if the gulls had their wings clipped and had been unable to. Either way, Cass caught them by surprise when she hatched phase one of her escape plan.

She was undecided on how long she should linger. Hopefully one of them would slip up and spout out helpful information about the hawk they were chasing. They didn't seem to be the brightest of goons.

Frick cut off the edge of his flannel, wrapping the scrap around the bleeding, swollen finger. "You have to text her back." His voice was a sharp contrast to the tone he had while barking orders and threats. A timidness laced his tone now. Was he scared?

"Y-you do it."

He held up his crushed digit. "I can't unlock my cell phone. This is the fingerprint I need to open it, and it's mangled."

That's why we don't put our fingers where they don't belong. Cass was tempted to shift just so she could rain insults and sarcasm down on them. Maybe with a little luck, she'd drop her secret weapon—bird poop.

She was about to glance around for a closer beam to roost on when a commotion erupted outside. Numerous engines growled, and tires screeched into what she assumed was a parking lot next to the building.

Did FUC shift their ass into gear to come find her? Hopefully one of the stooges below would spill it in interrogation.

The one with all his fingers moved closer to a grimy window. "Shit. They found us!"

"Text Sandy now!"

"How'd they find us so fast?"

Because Grayson is the best hound agent there is, she thought smugly. She beamed with pride, puffing out the feathers on her chest. There wasn't a critter he couldn't track. He'd had massive potential as an agent when she met him a decade ago, but he'd needed to learn how to work in a team. It was clear he had that down now. He was more than a dog sniffing out a bad guy. He had a team of super-smart technicians behind him. They excelled at analyzing data and evidence—not that she'd admit that to any FUC personnel. They could be disorganized, bickering, and down-right silly, and Cass didn't know how Grayson could focus with all the FUCN'A chaos, but sometimes they ran as a well-oiled machine.

She was glad they were on their A-game today. Though she doubted her goose—or rather, peahen—would have been cooked without FUC rolling in.

The large barn-style doors rolled open. A handful of agents pilled in. Frack dropped his phone mid-text.

Grayson stood in the doorway, a silhouette with the faint glow of headlights behind him. He crossed his arms, narrowing his glance at the two men. "Where is she?" His voice was stern and flat. It wasn't a question but a command.

Cass' feathers ruffled as the heat pooled in her

belly. He was damn sexy when bossing people around. Especially when they were bad guys.

She was about to coo from the rafters when Frick pulled something out of his back pocket. A small metal device that fit in the palm of his hand. Grayson didn't notice. He was looking at the cages.

Frick took a step forward, raising his hand and the potential weapon.

I don't think so.

7

———————

Grayson eyed the chicken-wire cages. They were empty. So where was Cass? One of the men touted a bloody hand, and he feared Cass had injured him and was punished. If one of them so much as plucked a feather out of her beautiful body…

It happened so fast. One second the two men cowered in front of him and the other agents, the next… He wasn't even sure. The man with the beard started to raise his arm, and out of the air above them, a giant bird swooped down. Cass soared down with talons splayed. She raked her nails across the man's back, pushing him over with the momentum. As he fell to the ground, screaming in agony, an object flew from his uninjured hand, and Cass trotted after it.

Thank God Cass was safe!

Agents swarmed the men to cuff them, not

wanting to take any chances. Grayson realized that Cass had seen something he hadn't. But what was that small object?

He followed the trail the object left in the dust coating the floor when it slid across the concrete. A flat, rectangular device stuck out of a pile of yellow sawdust. At first glance, it appeared to be a remote of some kind. A handful of tiny, round buttons dotted its surface. He flagged an agent to come bag the device. He doubted it controlled a television. It was more likely a weapon. Had Cass not swooped out of the rafters, who knew what could have happened to him?

He looked to Cass as though she could give him an answer. She blinked at him with a large, round hazel eye before combing through her back feathers with her beak. With a shake, she ruffled up her grey plumage. The giant bird trilled loudly, the sound reverberating off the metal walls of the building. She opened her vast wingspan, staring at Grayson. If he didn't know any better, he'd think she was annoyed.

Then it hit him. He snapped his fingers. "Who has ASS Agent Sparks' clothes?" Cass had information she needed to tell him and was unable to communicate that in bird form.

A young agent ran outside to the waiting vehicles. Soon she was back in the warehouse carrying Cass' belongings in a large plastic bag. She found a cleaner area to set them down, away from the blood Cass had drawn from the henchman. The peahen clicked her beak in thanks.

She turned to Grayson with her wide bird eyes. He realized he was staring at her. He turned away as she shifted back into human form in a corner hidden from the view of others.

"Stare at me that long again and I'll charge you," Cass quipped with a chuckle as soon as she was back in human form. "Damn! It feels good to talk again!" Her voice was so bright that Grayson could hear the smile in it.

"I'm good."

Grayson turned as Cass was adjusting her pencil skirt over her generous curves. She stood barefoot in the dust, pulling her pink blouse down over a sheer camisole. "The hawk's name is Sandy. The crows were right. Partially." She shrugged.

"Did the goons say where she is?"

"It seemed she was on her way here to deal with me until FUC showed up." She glanced around at the empty cages. "I think they were in the process of relocating but hadn't found a new evil lair yet. One of the henchmen was mid-text when you busted through the door."

Grayson turned to one of the agents, Brett Kipp, collecting evidence. He beamed with pride, watching one of his former students hard at work in the field. Brett was about to scoop up another sample of sawdust when Grayson asked, "Do we have the cell phones from the men in custody?" Brett pointed to a box filled with baggies of various sizes.

"Are you any closer to finding the hawk that tried to kidnap Ellie?" Brett asked. Ellie was his girlfriend. They were on assignment together when she was taken.

Grayson nodded. "I'm going to roast that bird like a Thanksgiving turkey." Brett grinned before going back to collecting samples. It seemed his sloth smile followed him in human form. Grayson turned to the box, rummaging through it until he found a phone.

"Can you unlock this?" he asked, turning back to Brett before he could grab more evidence to bag and tag.

"Of course." The bright lights shimmered in his wavy, brown hair as he leaned back slightly to reach down toward his pants. "I have a DICC."

Grayson stared, his mouth hanging open. He cocked his head to the side, like a confused dog. He didn't understand what Brett's biological sex had to do with anything.

Brett rolled his eyes. "DICC, as in Data, Imagery, & Communications Collector." He fished a USB drive out of his pocket. "You should really be more up-to-date on newer technology, Agent Stone."

"Or we should come up with better acronyms that don't make it sound like you're hitting on me," he growled. Grayson knew all about the USB device that was capable of copying information from a computer or smartphone. He wanted to add that DICC and dick sounded *exactly* the same, however, he decided to hold his tongue. "Can you please use your"—he paused—"DICC to copy the information from the phone?"

Brett nodded. "You betcha!" He went to work as fast as a sloth-shifter could. If anyone wanted to find the red-tailed hawk shifter more than Grayson, it was Brett. Probably Ellie, too.

Cass' heels clacked on the concrete as she sauntered over. "Do you think we can get the phone number of Sandy and trace it?"

"I'm hoping for more than that." Grayson watched Brett as he worked. With any luck, there would be saved locations in the henchman's map app. If they were in the process of finding a new nest for Sandy, maybe it was stored in the phone.

"I think Sandy hires for brawn and not brains. There's probably a lot on those phones that shouldn't be." Cass narrowed her hazel eyes to slits. He wanted to ask if she was all right, but the Cass he remembered didn't respond well to emotional displays.

Brett placed his DICC next to the phone and waited for the information to copy over. He then pulled over a briefcase carrying his laptop. After pushing the USB into the computer, he opened the file, his fingers taking the time to intentionally find the key they were looking for. Grayson balled his hands into tight fists, trying his best to redirect the energy his brain was sending to tap his foot. Brett was helping as fast as he could. He didn't want to appear rude.

"What are you hoping for, Agent Stone?" Brett glanced up.

"Saved locations from the map function. Also send all the text messages to one of our techies at WANC. Have them pay close attention to any communications with someone named Sandy."

Brett nodded. "I'm securely emailing the encrypted file now. Only you and the receiving agent at WANC can open it with the password."

Grayson said his thanks. He opened the email and frowned. "Looks like we have a lot to comb through."

Cass glanced down at Grayson's phone. "How do you want to run this? Should we split up?"

"We're never splitting up again." Worry tainted his tone of voice. They'd lucked out this time. Cass was as fine as the feathers on a peacock's train. Next time, she could be unable to form sentences like the flock of seagulls from the park. Who knew if that damage was reversible.

She put her hands on her hips, tapping her nails. The gems caught the light, reflecting tiny rainbows all over his shirt and the floor. "I'm fine."

"Good." He took her word for it, though didn't fully believe her. Luckily the goons were bumbling idiots, but it still must have been terrifying for Cass at times. "We need to be extra careful in the future.

This Sandy is no one to be trifled with. My student barely escaped. And the gulls..." His voice caught in his throat. It was too thick and heavy to make speech. The thought of something terrible happening to Cass... He couldn't bear it.

Her eyes widened. The lights above reflected in them like tiny stars, burning with the brilliance and spark that was Cass. Her face softened, a delicate flower. He wanted to scoop her up in his arms and taste her sweetness.

"I can take care of myself," she reassured him softly.

"You shouldn't have to do it alone."

He felt stuck in an anthill. The various agents toiled around them, collecting samples, taking pictures, writing notes. But for him, the world stood still. They all faded away until he and Cass were all that remained. The fire that had been extinguished years ago was relit. It smoldered, urging him to finish this tonight. Find Sandy and put the whole thing to rest. Then he could focus on whatever remained between him and Cass.

Instead, he said, "I should take you to WANC to be evaluated."

Cass blinked. Her long lashes fluttered in confusion. "I don't need to be looked over." Her voice was flat and emotionless, the usual walls she kept up back in place.

"We should call it a night. Start fresh in the morning. Let me take you to your hotel at least." He tried to show how important she was to him. He wanted to protect her. They were up against a foe who experimented on bird shifters, leaving them mutated. Who knew how close Cass had just been to that fate?

"Did you drive my car here?" She tapped her foot on the ground. He debated changing the subject. He'd been scolded in the past for touching her car, but Cass would find out eventually, so he decided to come clean.

He nodded. "It was the fastest way to get here."

"If there's one scratch…" Instead of letting him have it, she winked.

Grayson was taken aback. The old Cass would have reamed him out for touching her stuff. Especially her sacred car. But instead, she joked with him. This *was* a new Cass. And he was curious to find out what else about her might have changed.

"Do you want to grab a bite to eat?" he asked, deciding there was one way to find out.

Cass didn't know what to say. Was Grayson worried about her, or had her mind created what she wanted to see in his words and his gestures? She wanted so badly to believe he cared, but perhaps it was just protocol. *I should take you to WANC to be evaluated.*

When she refused, she thought he'd insist, but

instead, he invited her out to dinner. She stared at him in confusion, not knowing what to make of it.

"I am hungry," she admitted, her stomach rumbling. She'd think more about it later. Right now, she needed to eat. Her brain didn't function well when hangry.

Grayson held out her keys. "I'll let you drive."

She could tell by the look on his face he'd prefer if she didn't. It wasn't a secret that he hated her driving. She hesitated on snatching the keys from his hand. Yes, she loved to drive, and, yes, she preferred to be in control… but she could let someone else drive for once, right? It was Grayson, after all. If he didn't crash the car speeding to rescue her, she was sure he'd be careful on the way to the restaurant. "Why don't you? I could use the break."

Grayson raised an eyebrow but didn't question her decision. He closed his hand around the keys. Turning on his heels, he led Cass into the floodlights and headlights of the FUC agent vehicles. She smiled to herself. If Grayson needed another sign that she'd changed, she hoped this was it.

8

Surprise still rocked Grayson's brain as he drove Cass' car toward a nearby restaurant. She hadn't chided him for taking her car without asking to the building where she was being held. Then she allowed him to drive to the restaurant. Neither of those facts matched the image he had of Cass in his mind.

Grayson wanted to believe she'd matured, but nagging doubt rippled through him. Did it matter if she'd evolved? Just because she showed up a changed woman didn't mean that she wanted to give their relationship another try. He needed to be careful. It was too easy to fall for her, and he couldn't let that happen. He didn't want to be hurt again. Entertaining the idea of Cass and him getting back together would be playing with fire.

He chanced glances at her as he drove, seeing that her face remained neutral as she recounted the day's events, everything from the two bozos who kidnapped her from the park to what happened where she was being held. He remained silent, allowing her the space to express herself and get it off her chest.

"I'm not traumatized," she reassured him after he asked if she was all right. Again. "Maybe I'm a little afraid of what's on the bottom of my stilettos after we went to the bird bar, but..."

He turned toward the restaurant and parked the car in the lot. "Cass."

"What?" She stared at him, biting her full bottom lip, her eyes widened with surprise.

"It's okay to not be okay."

"I don't know what you mean." She shrugged and picked up her handbag, but before she could leave the car, he continued.

"You seem so level after the encounter with the henchmen. Even if you're fine with being captured, they still threatened to mutate you like the gulls."

"I almost bit one of their fingers off." The grin that accompanied her shrug didn't fully meet her eyes. From what he knew of Cass and her background, her mother hadn't raised her to be able to fully express herself or her feelings. He'd hate if she was holding it in now.

"In self-defense," he agreed. "But I know how I feel when I react in the field. Mixed feelings are normal."

Something stirred behind her eyes. Her skin wrinkled around her mouth as she assessed him. She sucked in a deep breath, leaning back in the bucket seat of her car. The leather whined beneath her as she shifted her weight. He braced himself for her to unload, but as quickly as her walls tumbled down, they were put back up.

Cass straightened, plastering a smile on her face. "I told you, I'm fine."

Grayson nodded, deciding to drop it. He'd reached out an olive branch and gave her permission to feel, but maybe that wasn't what she needed.

"Let's go in and eat." Exhaustion crippled his excitement about dinner with Cass. Anxiety weaved a boulder in the pit of his stomach. Despite everything, he'd really hoped that something might come out of this mission—something beyond just catching the red-tailed hawk who'd kidnapped Ellie.

He'd foolishly thought that maybe something could be repaired between himself and Cass.

Instead of surrendering to self-doubt, he opened the car door and got out, leading Cass to the restaurant.

Cass felt she was under a microscope. After the crash years ago, if she heard one more person ask if she was okay or say they were sorry, she thought she'd scream. Now Gray was treating her like a fragile glass vase. They were nice to look at, but you wouldn't dare play football with them. Like she was only good enough to be a paper pusher, not tough enough for fieldwork. Cass felt she'd more than proved herself years ago.

She sat opposite him at the corner booth in the back of the busy restaurant. The scents of fried food and tomato sauce paraded past her as a waiter walked by with a tray. Without glancing up at her, Grayson pulled over his menu, burying his face in it.

What was that about in the car? She swallowed the words before temptation overcame her to spew them. One second, he was all business, and the next, he was concerned for her safety, more than a partner on a job. Cass couldn't tell if Gray wanted to rekindle things between them or if he was just doing his job. She wanted to know his motives. Was there more growing between them? Or was her mind playing tricks on her? She decided upon a rephrase. "Why are you concerned about me?"

Grayson was about to answer when the waitress appeared for their drink order. He asked for water, hardly glancing up. Was he afraid to look at her? Cass ordered red wine before the employee left. She studied what little she could see of Gray's face, waiting for an answer.

He put the menu down, locking eyes with her. "When you disappeared, I feared the worse." She was about to brush off his concern when he interrupted, "Cass, those seagull shifters were in bad shape. You could be doing nothing more than muttering my name right now." His eyebrows lifted, opening his face into an expression of concern.

All those words she cut him to the bone with years ago and he still feared for her safety. It made her feel worse. He was a gem, and she'd treated him like shit. He was a nice enough person to still care at the end of the day if an evil scientist turned her brain to mush. She had a lot of making up to do for what she'd done if she hoped they could be anything like friends someday. As far as anything more than friends? She knew better than to dream of that.

"I'm sorry." She buried her face in her own menu, afraid for her vulnerability to show.

"You were only trying to get a lead on the case."

"No. For Toronto." There. She'd said it. After over a decade. And she felt like shit for not apologizing sooner.

Grayson's mouth hung open. He'd inhaled sharply as if about to speak when the waitress dropped their drinks in front of them. He smiled up at her in thanks. Cass picked up the wine nearly mid-air. The tart tang of the fermented grapes danced on the back of her tongue. A dark flavor that matched her mood.

She shook her head. "I should've told my mother to fuck off."

"Cass, she led you to believe people were only as good as they looked."

She laughed bitterly, shaking her head. His words were venom. It was a hard pill to swallow. "Then I broke my face, and the only rules I knew about the world didn't make sense anymore."

It was the first time she'd spoken aloud about the emotional scarring of the crash. For so long she thought if she didn't voice it, some of what bounced around in her skull hadn't happened. She had gone from beauty queen to disfigured in an instant, and when her own mother visited her in the hospital, she screamed before fainting.

Cass stared at the restaurant wall while the memory singed within her. Though she'd grown from that moment, it still stung. It was barbed wire curled around her psyche, squeezing tight whenever the flashback surfaced. Raw and stinging.

"Broke your…" Grayson blinked, clearly trying to make sense of the small morsel of information she'd shared. "Your mother couldn't possibly…" Grayson didn't finish the question.

"She acted like I was dead," she filled in. "Me being alive wasn't a blessing to her; it was a curse. All her hard work down the drain." Cass' words were clipped with venomous anger. She'd wanted so badly to tell her mother how she felt after her reaction in the hospital, after all that was said. But she'd kept it in, fermenting in her soul. A poison that separated her from her mother. She tasted that bitterness whenever she thought of calling Mother to check in.

"How could she treat her own daughter like that?" Grayson asked with warmth in his voice and eyes.

"Mother never gave a shit about who I was as a person or what my feelings were." Cass closed her eyes. How she wished she could have had Grayson by her side during her recovery instead of pushing away someone who could have been part of her support system. At least she'd had Bianca. Without her, Cass would have had no one to hold her up after the crash. "When I accepted that, a lot of things made sense."

"That doesn't mean it doesn't hurt."

Cass tilted her head to the side. "True. It sucks. But I know what to expect from her now." The lets-get-coffee-and-talk-about-your-feelings-so-I-can-support-you mom wasn't what Cass'd known. It was more like, "beauty is painful, get over it." Instead of "sorry your face is fucked up," she got, "I told you playing agent would screw your chances of competing again." After Cass' mom left the hospital that first day, Cass started to fear Mother had been right, that Cass had been selfish for joining ASS. That her need to make a difference, her yearning to be known for more than being a ditzy beauty queen, and her determination to show how much she had to offer the world, had just been a faze.

"You two still talk?"

"Yeah. But not about anything important unless I want to leave pissed off."

Grayson paused, chewing on his next question. "Why do you still talk to her?"

Cass understood his pause. This was a sensitive conversation. Back in the day, she'd have verbally ripped his head off for less. After months of therapy —physical and mental— Cass realized she protected herself with a prickly exterior, lashing out with words if anyone threatened to crack the delicate mask she wore in public. "I don't know," she admitted breathlessly. The power behind her voice felt snatched by their topic of conversation. She was beat. Maybe Gray was right. Once that tough exterior split, the layers within crumbled, exposing a deep well of trauma at her core. It was a part of her that Cass pretended didn't exist until it reared its ugly head and she couldn't ignore it.

The waitress appeared, ready to take their order. "We can talk about it later if you want," Grayson offered.

"We'll take a brief time out." Cass wanting anything but. She wanted to get it all out. But first, they'd satisfy the waitress. They paused the conversation long enough to order their meals and then continued.

Cass closed her eyes as the restaurant employee left, her mind flooding with images from the hospital, being stuck in bed. And her mother's face. She shook her head, clearing her thoughts to try to find the best way to start. "It wasn't all bad. Healing from the crash."

"A crash." Gray eyed the scar above her left eye, slicing through her brow. Shifters were usually quick to heal. She could see the questions he was afraid to ask forming behind his kind brown eyes. "I'd heard you were out of the field for a while, but I never imagined you'd been harmed. I thought maybe you'd gone undercover or maybe you'd taken time off to spend time with your family. Or… that you'd found someone…"

"I was in a high-speed car chase," she quickly interjected, hating the way his voice broke on the last words. "I lost control of the car and hit a pole. It wasn't just my face that got crushed but my pelvis too, and I had lots of cuts and wounds all over my body. My car had been sabotaged, and my airbags didn't deploy."

"Holy shit," Gray breathed.

She nodded. "What I didn't know was the perps sprayed me with some type of bioweapon that halted my ability to heal. I recuperated like a human would. I still heal slower now than I used to."

"I'm missing the 'not all bad' part," Grayson said gruffly, his eyes wide as he listened to her traumatic story.

"I mean there were some really dark days at first, but then my determination to live, to survive, kicked in. Part of that was looking for the good around me."

"Such as?" He looked as if he couldn't imagine anyone finding a bright side in such a situation—but especially not someone like Cass.

"Well, such as Bianca, my friend since childhood. We hadn't been very close for a long time, but she showed up when I most needed her, and she became a huge support. We grew closer. She gave me hope, and I learned to heal and grow. Not just from the physical injuries but to be a whole person." Cass wondered why her friend had stuck it out so long with her. Maybe one day she would ask.

"I'm glad you had someone with you, seeing as your mother..."

"Walked out on me." Cass nodded in confirmation. "But that was good too. Because she did that, I was able to see her for who she truly is and leave behind all the bullshit she'd been feeding me all those years. Without that crash"—she paused, thinking on her words while tears stung her eyes and she fought to hold them back—"I think I'd still be the same cruel, shallow person I was all along."

"I don't believe that. I think it would have taken you longer to get here, but I know you would have changed."

Cass wished she could believe that. Gray always saw the best in people. There was no way to alter reality to see if he was correct.

Needing a break from the intensity of the topic, she smiled and changed the subject. "So, you're a FUCN'A instructor now?"

To her immense relief, Grayson allowed the new topic as the waitress placed their plates of food before them. Throughout the entire meal he didn't bring up her accident or scars again, sparing her from having to discuss the chapter of her life she was finally walking away from.

9

———

Grayson lumbered back to the car, his full belly weighing him down. The juicy, certified non-shifter steak he ate had been incredibly delicious. After some convincing, he agreed to let Cass drop him off at WANC, though his protective instinct still loomed, not wanting to let her go off on her own.

He had to let that go. She wasn't his to protect, and even with her new scars, she wasn't someone who *needed* his protection. Better to turn his mind to the paperwork he needed to file before leaving for the night.

"Do you think any of those map leads from the cell phone will pan out?" Cass asked as she pulled the car out of the restaurant parking lot.

"I hope so." He didn't want to overpromise anything. "It seems a good chance we'll find something with the crow gang talking about a Sandy or

Cindy down at the park and the goons who took you mentioning a Sandy. They seem like the type of baddies who would save the location of their evil lair on their cell phones."

"Don't you think this Sandy flew the coop after we picked up Frick and Frack?"

"Their warning text message didn't get sent before we raided the place. I'm hoping she has no idea they were captured."

Cass nodded but didn't look convinced.

"I have an agent assigned to monitor the phone. If Sandy sends them a message, they will respond accordingly," Grayson reassured her. Cass was right to worry. Normally they would have been working into the night, following leads. Grayson shut that down out of worry for her well-being, knowing that mistakes could be made when agents weren't at their best. He was running point on this investigation, and if he made a call that put Cass in danger again, he'd never forgive himself. He was fine with calling it a night and potentially slowing down the investigation if it ensured Cass' safety.

"What would a hawk shifter want with a cat?" Cass asked softly.

Grayson assumed that question was rhetorical but proposed an answer. "We know the hawk did mercenary work for money, but it's not a stretch to assume a low-level lackey would want to move up. Especially knowing how smart hawks can be."

"They're not content to work underneath a boss forever. I wonder if what she's involved in now was always her end goal." Cass rubbed the scar on her eyebrow as she thought.

"We've seen it before, a henchman for hire using each job to gain knowledge, experience, and funds before going out on their own."

"Your file said that the red-tailed hawk worked for Dr. Smith. After he was killed by Ellie—"

"In self-defense," Grayson interjected.

"Ellie defended herself and put Dr. Smith out of commission," Cass corrected. "Then, Sandy—assuming Sandy and the red-tailed hawk are one and the same—was open for self-employment."

"Right." He wondered if she had a hypothesis, if she saw something he hadn't.

"So again, that goes back to my question, what did they want with a cat?" Cass pursed her full lips as she thought. "The report didn't go in-depth about her, but it did mention she had previously been a rescued experiment and that experimentation had left her with special abilities."

"Right." Grayson nodded. "Ellie can bend light around herself to appear invisible."

"So Dr. Smith didn't want a cat, but he wanted the experiment who had that ability. Whatever his intentions with her were, it could be entirely possible that the hawk is picking up where Smith left off."

Grayson had no answers. He knew Cass didn't

need them. She was proposing questions to get him thinking. "Maybe we'll find out tomorrow."

During dinner, Grayson had chatted happily away about his new career as an instructor, and while she'd been glad for the reprieve from talking about herself, she couldn't help but regret that any chance at romance seemed to fizzle out.

The car ride back to FUCN'A was completely business. They chatted about the case, keeping the conversation safe and off themselves. Cass wasn't sure if she should pursue it further or give up and talk about work. To be safe, she kept it all business.

She parked her car in the near-empty lot at WANC.

"I have to finish up some paperwork inside." Grayson paused, locking eyes with her. It sounded like an invitation.

Grayson had been shy back in the day when it came to women. If he was the same now, Cass couldn't be sure if he was hinting that he wanted her to come with him. Why couldn't he say what he wanted? It was strange that they'd once been so close, so able to tell each other exactly what they wanted, and now they were almost strangers. She had only herself to blame, after she'd hurt him so badly and let so many years go by without so much as a phone call to check in with him.

"Do you need help?" She tested the waters, prodded for his intention.

"If you want to." He shrugged. "I could use the company." Subtle, though more direct than before. But still not committed. He was keeping himself safe.

Cass wouldn't waste the invitation, tentative as it was. She didn't want to leave him. Not yet. Dinner had been so nice. A well-earned distraction. When she took this mission, she thought she wanted to prove she was different. A new and improved Cass. But now she wanted more. That surprised her. The feelings for Gray from long ago bubbled up. Despite telling herself over and over that she'd come to FUCN'A with no expectations, she couldn't deny that she wanted nothing more than for things between them to heat up again.

The thing was she wasn't sure if she deserved it. She may have changed, but that didn't mean she didn't still need to pay penance for how she'd treated Gray the last time they worked together. It ate at her; a simmering guilt wedged deep in her gut. Because of it, she couldn't be certain if she was perusing him because she wanted another chance for a relationship or because she wanted his approval to erase her guilt over her behavior years ago. Cass wanted to be sure of her motives before she made a move. Right now, she was testing him and herself.

She couldn't bear the thought of breaking his heart again.

She'd told herself he was "the one that got away," but in reality, she'd driven him away, and she had to live with that. Mend all the ugly bits inside herself. And she didn't mean the scars from the wreckage that left her mangled. There were personality wounds from her childhood that needed healing. Defense mechanisms to weed out and replace with healthier responses. Recovery and growth that had to be done before she could be worthy of a man like Grayson.

She followed him through the parking lot and toward the building. To the side, crickets sang in the grass of the campus, a serenade against the backdrop of a sky sprinkled with stars.

Grayson held the doors to the main building open for her, and they wound through the empty halls toward his office. Most of the agents had cleared out for the night. A few lingered behind, clacking at their computers.

"The nocturnal shifters usually have classes in the sub-floors," he explained. "They like windowless rooms in case they happen to work past sunrise."

She nodded, suddenly unsure of what to say.

When they arrived at his office, Grayson immediately settled in behind his computer and logged on. He glanced up at her after typing something in. "You look worried. Is everything okay?"

Based on his earlier lines of questioning, Cass figured he was probably wondering if the day's events were finally getting to her. Telling him that was the case would almost be an easy out, but she opted for the truth. "I'm wondering where we'd be if I hadn't been such an ass back then."

"You'll always be ASS, Cass." He gave her a crooked smile. "Once an ASS agent, always an ASS agent, but FUCN'A always welcomes your kind as instructors, if that's what you're thinking about."

She appreciated his effort at levity, but Pandora's box had been opened, and she had to see it through. "You know what I mean. If I'd been a better person back then, if I'd been better to you… If we'd… been able to stay together."

His eyebrows wrinkled as he reflected. "I don't think we'll ever be able to answer that question," he mused softly. He kept his attention on her, no longer focused on the report and the computer before him.

Did that mean he'd closed the door on the idea of getting back together? Fear gnawed at Cass' stomach. She could face down foes intent on killing her in the field, but the thought of having a heart-to-heart about her feelings was nauseating. She rubbed the building sweat of her palms onto her skirt, trying to pass it off as adjusting a wrinkle.

He continued to watch her movements as if they could help read her mind. He scratched at the stubble forming on his jaw. Silently assessing. Looking as though he were trying to figure her out.

Cass chose her next words closely. "I am so mad at myself for how I treated you."

"Good."

She winced at the honesty but held strong. Old Cass would have bit back, felt the need to defend herself, but now… Now she was the kind of person who could take accountability and apologize when she needed to. "Even after I said it. I knew it was wrong. But I did nothing to change it until after the crash."

Grayson said nothing, taking it all in.

Cass continued. "I had never realized how ugly I was on the inside—before the crash I mean— until my mom screamed like that. You'd think she'd be relieved I was alive; instead, she only cared for my looks." She swallowed. "It was looking into a mirror for the first time. Seeing her true self showed me how the outside world saw *me*. I saw how I was to others for the first time. And I didn't like it." It felt good getting it off her chest. A weight lifted.

After a moment of silence, he spoke. "I really hate knowing this happened to you and I wasn't there for you. Despite what happened between us, despite the hurt, I still would have wanted to be there for you." His face wrinkled in concern.

She sighed in relief. Those words told her everything she needed to know: Grayson didn't hate her.

"After how I treated you, I didn't deserve a friend like you." Her voice grew thick in her throat as tears threatened to fall.

"You have to forgive yourself." He spoke in a soft voice. A forgiving, *caring* voice. "That was so long ago, and what really matters is who you are now. That you've managed to grow. You didn't have to change, but you did."

Cass collapsed into the chair across from Grayson's desk. She crumpled like a wilting flower, falling apart at the seams. She never knew what was missing until now. She needed his *permission* to forgive herself. Tears rolled down her warm cheeks. Instead of etching sadness on her face, it was a display of relief.

Then he was there, by her side, handing her a tissue. Steady, reliable, loyal Grayson, taking care of her like he always had. She blew her nose before accepting the offer he gave her by way of his outstretched arms. She burrowed into the soft fabric of his flannel shirt, overcome with emotion as his muscular arms wrapped around her. His hand cupped the back of her head, stroking her curls.

Cass dabbed at her wet eyes with a new tissue. It would take far more than some hot tears to smudge her waterproof makeup, but she didn't want to look a soggy mess.

"Thank you."

"For what?" he asked, brushing coils of hair out of her face.

"For being you." She smiled at him. Her fingers traced the line of his jaw. How did a man like Gray exist? Not only was he rugged and manly but he also was tender and thoughtful. He didn't shy away from discussing his feelings. He was also the first to stand up for what was right. It's what had drawn him to FUC. Protecting shifters. Catching bad people. And giving others hope.

After all of Cass' fears and insecurities melted, she was left with the fact that she did want him. She loved Gray for being Gray. And for believing the best in her when she showed him the worst.

She leaned forward and pressed her lips to his cheek. His soothing scent greeted her, a comforting mix of musky aftershave and fresh woody air. Gray nuzzled her neck, his warmth caressing her. His soft lips followed the line of her neck to the curve of her jaw, leaving kisses in their wake. Heat flowed from them, tingling under her skin. Goosebumps erupted on her arms. Her body loved his touch. It responded to him in a way she never thought possible. She'd had casual sex before, but it was always different with Grayson. Her soul came alive around him.

When their lips met, Cass' heart rejoiced. He parted his mouth, inviting her in. Her tongue wrapped around his, pulsing and stroking. He tasted of home. Not the one where she came from but the one she wished to cultivate. She craved that sense of belonging.

Gray's large hands explored her body as she caressed his muscular back. His lips roamed back down her neck, licking and kissing. Her nipples tingled as he unbuttoned her blouse, his hands cupping her supple breasts. His mouth found one, twirling his tongue around her nipple before sucking it in. A pooling of moisture wet her panties. As if scenting it, Gray ran a warm hand up her thigh toward her waiting pussy. He kneeled before her, worshipping her with his mouth and hands.

He unzipped her skirt. She shimmied out of it, leaning back in the chair. The cooler air of the office kissed her skin. It tingled where more goosebumps formed.

Grayson slid down her lace panties, exposing her delicate skin. The hot kisses meandered down her abdomen, sending ripples of excitement through her body. He dipped his tongue inside her before sucking at her clitoris. Her muscles tensed with the building climax inside her. He slipped a finger inside while twirling his tongue around the tiny fold of flesh. Her vagina tensed around it, ready for his cock. She needed him inside her, yearned for his body pressed against hers. He fluttered his fingers inside her, her muscles squeezing as her climax mounted. Her breath quickened with her racing heart. Gray's fingers and mouth worked in a steady rhythm. Cass' orgasm flowed, releasing the tension from her body. Her legs shook until exhaustion set in.

She wanted more, but damn was she tired.

Grayson looked up at her with his soft brown eyes. "Why don't I forget about this paperwork and we go back to my place?"

The offer enticed Cass. She pictured all the kinky things they could do in the privacy of his home. Hell, what did that matter? She was half-clothed, and his office door was open.

"I would like that," she agreed, buttoning back up her shirt. She wondered how long their clothes would stay on once at Gray's place.

10

Gray smiled at Cass as she opened her eyes in the light of the morning sun. The night before they'd had enough sex to make a rabbit shifter proud. And everywhere. They hardly made it in the door of his house before going at it again in the entry hallway. Then again on the kitchen table. And in the shower, before finally making it to bed. To have more sex. Gray never had so much sex in one night before, not even when he and Cass had been at their hot and heaviest years ago. Now, he'd figured he'd be too old for that sort of thing. They'd proved that wrong last night.

Cass' eyes were nothing more than slits lined with smudges and flakes of black. Since she didn't plan on spending the night, she only had what Gray could offer in his medicine cabinet to wash the makeup off her face. She looked like a transforming raccoon shifter. Grayson stifled a chuckle. "Do you want breakfast?" he asked. Cass looked like she wanted to roll over and go back to sleep. Her tired eyes barely opened. Instead, she nodded.

Grayson popped out of bed, throwing on a pair of sweatpants that were crumpled in a heap on his bedroom floor. Cass groaned as he peered out of the bedroom curtains, a ribbon of light touching her face. She flopped an arm over her eyes to shield her from the bright sunlight.

"I'll wake you when the food's ready."

Cass grunted a response he assumed was agreement.

Grayson strolled down the hall towards the kitchen. He flipped on the radio, playing soft music as he worked. Breakfast was important in his family. Many fond memories centered around the meal. Soon the pan was sizzling with certified non-shifter bacon and eggs. Chunks of seasoned potato chunks sputtered in another pan. It smelled delicious. It smelled of home.

A blast of water sounded down the hall, emanating from the master bathroom. Cass had probably glimpsed the remnants of eyeliner and flaking mascara on her face and decided to give fixing it another go. After a few minutes, she sauntered down the hallway with a clean face, wearing one of his button-down flannels. The bottom hem of the shirt nearly reached the knees of her short frame.

Without her usual stilettos, Cass was significantly shorter than him. She raised her arms in a long stretch as she yawned.

"Smells good," she complimented him, taking a seat on one of the stools at the breakfast bar. The morning sun lit up flecks of short scars across her cheeks. The other day, Grayson had only noticed the one interrupting the hair of her eyebrow. The rest must have been masked by her foundation and concealer. In any case, he didn't think she was any less beautiful for them.

"Thanks," he said, grinning broadly. "The potatoes are my mother's recipe."

A dark expression clouded Cass' eyes for a moment. Grayson assumed it was the mention of a healthy relationship with his mother. He knew Cass yearned for that, had tried hard to get that with her own mom. He thought back to how Cass said her mom reacted to her injuries in the hospital. It chilled him to his core. Cass needed the support of friends and family with the kind of extensive injuries she'd described, and instead of a caring and helpful family member, she was cascaded with negativity. Rejection. But Cass powered through all that with her own sheer will.

"I would love to meet her," Cass said softly.

Grayson leaned forward, planting a kiss on her forehead. "I'd like that."

It was hard—no, near impossible—to peel themselves out of Gray's house after breakfast to get back to work. The temptation to make love again was strong. Cass wanted to wrap around his hard cock and ride him until the sun set. But they had an evil hawk to catch. Sex could wait; the opportunity to track down Sandy would not.

They reviewed the map locations while eating, deciding which areas were most likely to house a new evil lair for the experiments Sandy enjoyed. It was disgusting that a shifter could put another through such agony. And for what? Merging abilities? Learning about how shifting worked? Whatever the purpose, the methods were unethical. The ends did not justify the means in Cass' opinion. Many agreed. Hell, it was one of the few subjects FUC and ASS could see eye to eye on.

Once they planned out their day at Gray's breakfast bar, Cass slid out of his shirt and put her garments from yesterday back on. Aside from her thong, which she'd left in a crumpled heap in Gray's living room, abandoned during their sex sessions last night. It took her twenty minutes to track her bra down. That was hanging from the ceiling fan. Once she was able to get dressed, it was back to business. Since they left her car at WANC in their excitement to get back to Gray's, they decided it would save them time now to just go from his apartment to the locations of interest that had been pulled from the phones of Frick and Frack.

They had a lot of driving to do since the locations were in different towns across the area, and for once, Cass didn't mind letting Gray drive. In fact, it felt comfortable having him behind the wheel, going at his calm and patient speed.

After they found nothing out of the ordinary at the first two locations, Cass was beginning to think this was a wild goose chase. This was going to be a long, annoying day if nothing came of their investigation. Grayson eased his SUV into a parking space at the third location, an abandoned mall. Tufts of long grass and weeds sprouted up through the broken asphalt, running through the lot like exposed veins. The expanse of the mall stood in the distance, the glass of its doors cracked. No light escaped from inside the structure. It appeared forgotten.

Cass got out of the car and lifted her sunglasses for a better look. She leaned her elbows on the open vehicle door in front of her. "This place has seen better days," she mused. Patches of stucco on the outside walls had crumbled, falling off in tiny piles littered around the building. The mall had been abandoned for years. There were talks of turning it into office space, but the plans were never approved. Instead, the building sat aging and uncared for, becoming more and more derelict as time marched on. Cass wished she could say she had fond memories of malls in general, but every time her mom took her shopping, it was all business. Either they were dress or shoe shopping for an upcoming competition or her mom was scanning for new fashion trends for her own wardrobe. It always felt more like a chore during their outings, her mother's judgments and negativity killing off any scrap of fun.

A flock of seagulls lingered in a far corner of the lot, pecking at the ground and squawking. Cass couldn't help but think back to the unfortunate people from the park. She wondered if the hawk tried something to make the shifters' animal form more dominant, or spliced non-shifter humans with animals. Unfortunately, it was probably a little bit of both. Whatever she tried, the results were disastrous. Cass hoped FUCN'A could help them. So far, they hadn't heard any updates on that progress, but she kept hoping the results of the experiment were reversible. But what was Sandy's endgame? Was there a diabolical reason for her tests, or were they random?

Grayson nodded, his eyes scanning the mall. "It looks abandoned but be careful. This is the type of place that would make a great hideout." He sniffed at the gentle breeze, wrinkling his nose as he dissected the smells. "I should shift so my olfactory sense is more precise and sensitive."

A tingling filled Cass' stomach, heating up her

pussy as she thought about Gray taking his clothes off. Her eyes glided over the rock-hard muscles that were covered in clothes. Her lips pulled back in a mischievous smile, one that promised all the dirty things she wanted to do with him later.

He glanced her way as if reading her thoughts. "We'll have time for that later. Right now, we need to focus."

"All right," she agreed. "But a girl can dream." She chucked her sunglasses on the seat of Gray's SUV and closed the door, leaving her purse under the seat. Her handbag had been through enough on this case already. She thought back to the gross bird bar where their adventure started. Her shoes would have to hold out a bit longer.

Grayson glanced around the empty lot. They'd parked at the back entrance of the mall, nestled between a forest and a doctor's office that appeared to be closed for the day. The main road lay on the opposite side of the mall. Cass knew he didn't want to risk needing a COOCHI. She knew how Gray felt about paperwork.

Quickly Gray stripped down, throwing his clothes in an unorganized pile on the driver's seat. Then his body started the transformation. He seamlessly crouched down onto all fours during the process. Cass was amazed by his ability to balance. Even though, in her animal form, she remained with two legs instead of four, she struggled with acclimating to her giant bird body after shifting. It took a second to adjust where her weight sat in the new form. Gray didn't seem to have an issue at all. In a second, he padded on four massive paws toward the entrance of the mall. His brown nose hovered along the asphalt. The long, brown, velvet ears of his Basset Hound form flopped forward, wafting the various scents toward his waiting nostrils.

Cass watched in fascination. She always loved watching him work, especially in dog form. She wondered how her shifter senses differed from his.

She walked to the driver's side, reaching for Gray's backpack in the backseat. Cass piled his clothes inside before strapping it on his back—the entire activity something they'd done so many times before when they'd been partnered.

Gray assisted, picking up a paw at a time so Cass could put a strap around each front leg. It would ensure Grayson would have a set of clothes inside the mall if needed. It was a necessary precaution to avoid random sightings of naked people. A majority of streakers were shifters caught without their clothing or access to a NAKED—Network for Apparel and Kit Express Delivery—package. She patted him on the back when the bag seemed sturdy and properly balanced on his back.

She followed Grayson to the entrance, telling him to take his time. She kept her own ears and eyes open for anything suspicious but figured it would be another fruitless endeavor. Once they reached the doors, she pulled hard on the handle, expecting the door to be locked. Instead, it opened. *That is surprising. Maybe this site won't be a pointless stop after all.*

Gray waddled his frame into the vestibule with his short legs. Cass hurried to the next set of glass doors to open for him. She glanced around for clues that would explain the unlocked door. Nothing seemed out of place for a vacant mall. The dark corridor ahead held empty storefronts, not evil laboratories.

A crash echoed in the distance. She was about to ask Gray if he'd heard it when a metal barrier snaked down in front of her, blocking the mall entrance and separating her from Grayson.

11

The clamoring metal shot down so fast that Grayson didn't know what had happened until it was too late. He glanced over his brown-spotted shoulder to see a silver barrier slam into the ground behind him. He wasn't sure if Cass was locked completely in the vestibule or if they were merely separated, as it was impossible to see through the blockade. One thing was for sure: he was damn certain the mall didn't originally come equipped with it.

Hot anger burned inside Grayson. He'd told Cass they wouldn't get separated. That apparently was a promise he couldn't keep. If anything happened to her, he couldn't forgive himself. Hearing about the details of the crash all those years ago broke his heart. She'd lucked out yesterday, but he didn't want Cass to endure something like that ever again.

He used his canine eyes to survey the dark

surroundings. They were evolved to help dogs see at night, but with little to no light around, he struggled to make out anything. Not having any options, Grayson trudged on in search of another exit or the red-tailed hawk shifter.

Banging sounded on the metal divider behind him. Cass was probably trying to get in. At least, by the noise, he could tell she was safe. For now anyway.

Too many smells mixed on the ground. Stale foods and multiple scents mingled in a confusing mess around him. It was a challenge to separate any of them. None were strong or stood out from the others. Grayson assumed they were old and not recent. But that didn't mean Sandy wasn't here. Maybe this wasn't the entrance she used. He would have to be careful.

Grayson noted some light near the end of the wide corridor up ahead. He turned the corner, going deeper into the mall. Shadows drifted along as light filtered down from the skylight above. Whether they were made by passing clouds above or someone inside, Grayson was unsure. He paused, sniffing at the air. His ears swayed with the motion, ushering new smells toward him. Something familiar. Feathers.

It brought him back to childhood, cleaning out the chicken coops for his parents back on the farm. But the place reeking of birds didn't mean this was Sandy's lair.

His hound eyes adjusted to the dim light. He scanned the vacant shops. Some naked mannequins sprawled about in the dark windows, limbs sprawled at awkward angles. Nothing seemed out of the ordinary. *Is this another dead end? Or an old hideout the hawk used in the past?*

His paw pads pressed into the cool, dusty tile. His nails clicked softly with each step. The banging from the outside door stopped. Either Cass was captured or trying to find another way in. He hoped for the latter.

This place was creepy. He hated not knowing what had happened to Cass. But he couldn't rush to rescue her in case this was a trap.

Feet scurried in the distance, sounding like a four-legged creature. A small one.

Grayson inhaled deeply, hoping his nose could decide. Whatever it was, it didn't come from his direction. He'd have to sniff and track alone until he caught its trail.

Cass gritted her teeth, banging on the metal in front of her until her fists stung. She'd kick at the divider if she wasn't afraid to ruin her stilettos and end up with broken toes. There was no way this barrier would lift by her throwing a fit. She was so frustrated. She hated when she didn't sense something coming. And this trap was a surprise.

She turned on her heel, hoping she could get out the way she came in. The first set of doors appeared unchanged. She tapped her toes on the floor, fearing a trap door would open up beneath her if she took a step. Nothing happened. She chuckled. "Stop being paranoid, Cass."

Satisfied this wasn't a ruse to capture her again, Cass took a step. She shifted her weight on the foot, inching forward. She shook her head. *A trap door. Who would build an evil lair under a mall? It's probably in one of the department sto—*

Before Cass could finish the thought, the floor started moving, taking her down. She kept her cool, staying away from the walls, afraid to get close to them. She'd seen too many horror flicks where people were not careful enough on elevators. She stood there helpless, crossing her arms, waiting for the ride to end. She glanced around for any sign of a switch she may have accidentally hit. Cass doubted she'd be that fortunate. Probably someone was on the other end controlling this thing.

I'm never hearing the end of this from Gray. She was two for two on being captured during this case. That wasn't a great track record.

About forty feet of concrete later, the floor stopped its slow descent with a *thud*. She pivoted, glancing around for a door. Nothing resembled a handle. Assuming there was a way out, she pressed on the wall in front of her. It slid to the side, exposing a long, dimly lit corridor. She kicked herself for leaving her phone in Gray's car and for not thinking to put his phone in his backpack. *How stupid.* Even without Grayson having his cell, if she had her phone, she could've texted him to tell him about the little trip she took. If he got back to his vehicle, he could've been able to get the message and know where she was. If she got service this far below ground. That was a lot of ifs.

Her only option was to exit. She wasn't sure if someone was corralling her along, but what choice did she have? Gray knew they were separated. He'd turn over every floor tile of the mall to find her.

A shiver trickled down her spine as Cass stepped off the platform. The air was notably cooler this far below ground. Her summer blazer did little to protect her from the chill.

The whole experience was screaming evil lair. Aside from the hidden elevator and below-ground bunker, her shifter senses didn't alert her to anything too out of the ordinary. Still, she kept her guard up, listening for any clues she wasn't alone. Nothing but the sound of her heels on the concrete echoed back.

The dank hall ended at a metal door. The cold handle bit into her palm as she wrenched it open.

Nothing could have prepared her for what she saw inside.

Grayson caught up to the unsuspecting mouse and pounced on it. It writhed at the end of its tail, his paw holding it in place. The creature was the size of an ordinary mouse, but that didn't mean anything. Most shifters became human-sized animals, like him; others did not. He thought to his former student Ellie. When she shifted, she was the size of an ordinary housecat.

He leaned forward, inspecting the rodent. It didn't appear to be a threat. Grayson was about to let it go when it grew in size. Its legs lengthened, the fur receding to smooth skin. The tail altogether disappeared. Soon a young boy curled up on the floor in front of him, shivering on the cool tiles. The kid was no more than ten years old.

He looked up into Gray's hound face, cocking his head to the side. His long brown hair fell in his face. "Do you mind? I'm trying to find my sister." The little guy had some attitude. Gray admired his confidence.

Gray shifted back into human form, not too keen on the both of them naked in a chilly, abandoned mall. But how else could he communicate? "I'm looking for my friend. We got separated."

The boy nodded, his blue eyes widening. "My sister was invited here last week and never came home."

Gray felt bad for the kid. After seeing what Sandy

was capable of, what hope was there that his sister was still coherent?

"It's too dangerous." He needed the boy to understand. It wasn't safe here for him. This wasn't a game. The stakes were pretty high.

"No," the boy said firmly. "It's not. They only take birds."

"Your sister's a bird?"

The boy nodded before pushing his long hair out of his eyes. "I'm a mouse, like my mom, and she's a crow—"

"Like your dad," Gray interrupted, thinking back to the bird bar where they interrogated the crow biker gang. They said one of their friends went missing at the park. Maybe it was the same bird.

The boy nodded. "He's missing too." He shifted his eyes to the tiled ground before wiping at them with the back of his hand. He gave a little sniff. "No one believes me that they're here."

"How do you know they only take birds?" Grayson flung his bookbag off his shoulder, zipped open the closure, and fished out his shirt.

"I've been here, inspecting every inch of this stupid mall looking for my sister. If they wanted me, they would have taken me by now." He hung his head in defeat. His shaggy hair flowed back in his face.

"Put your clothes back on," he ordered, noticing the boy was shivering. "You can wait in my car." He hoped Cass had left it unlocked as he asked.

"No," the boy said firmly.

"Look, kid…"

"Phineas."

"I know you want to find your family, but this is dangerous."

Phineas exhaled sharply with a hiss. "You think I don't know that? Like I'm just a stupid kid?"

"I don't mean it like that. I don't want anything happening to you," Grayson explained softly. He pulled his T-shirt over his head before slipping on his flannel. Phineas stared at him, crossing his arms in protest.

He had to go back outside anyway to notify FUC and ASS of the situation. Maybe on the way he could convince the boy to wait there while he went back in to find the others. With the information Phineas shared, Grayson figured Cass was captured. Again. They weren't merely separated like he'd hoped.

"Please go get your clothes and meet me back here. I have to go back out to my car to call for help, but I think I know how they took my friend. At least where." He'd keep his instructions vague and tell the kid he wasn't inviting him along for the ride later on. Otherwise, he'd probably never talk Phineas out of leaving the mall.

Phineas squinted at Grayson, weighing his options. "Fine," he said after a moment of deliberation before getting up to walk toward his waiting clothes.

12

———————

This can't be real. Cass' mouth hung open in disbelief as she stared at the underground forest before her. Chirping birds filled the treetops. Whether they were wild birds or shifters, she couldn't tell. This wasn't the hallway of labs and prison cells she'd expected. A brilliant light overhead emulated the sun. Now she knew why the elevator had taken her so far underground. This chamber needed room for the trees. Was this Sandy's lair? If so, how did she pull it off?

She hesitated to take a step forward. This wasn't some amusement park. It was the likely hideout of an evil scientist who experimented on shifters. Even though the view before her was beautiful, looks could be deceiving. Cass knew that more than anyone.

She was about to turn around to look for a hidden door in the hallway when a robin landed at her feet.

The bird looked up at her with one of its round yellow eyes. Then it opened its beak. Instead of a chirp coming out, it said one word. "Run."

Cass nearly fell over. She shut the door and turned. The bird had a human voice. It was similar to the seagulls in the park, shifters with a bizarre blend of human and animal traits. They seemed to not be able to control it. Was this what Sandy intended? Shifters who could talk in their animal form?

She ran down the corridor. Her heels slipped on the damp floor, threatening to slide her feet out from under her. She slowed up slightly, afraid to be thrown into the fake forest with the other mutated shifters if she fell. Maybe she was being watched. She didn't intend to stick around to find out.

Thankfully, the open elevator waited at the end of the hall. Cass expected the wall to close, locking her out. She hopped on, stamping her feet, trying to get the damn thing to work. Something *clicked* in the floor. The open wall in front of her slid closed. She stomped on the floor in various places until it started its ascent.

Cass froze, afraid to step on the wrong part of the floor. She glanced down, studying the rug to see what part she'd hit with her toe. She rolled the carpet up to find a series of buttons below. She must have accidentally hit one when she entered the mall with Grayson.

The slow elevator squeaked to a halt as she

reached the main entrance to the mall. The unfortunate barrier remained in front of her. She'd have to find a way to…

"Where the hell did you come from?" a familiar voice said behind her.

Cass whorled around to find Grayson standing at the entrance to the outside, a boy standing tall next to him, his slender arms plastered across his chest. He held open the exterior door to the building.

"A friend of yours?" she asked, eyeing the kid.

"I asked first." Grayson crossed his arms across his muscled chest.

"There's a forest about forty feet under the mall. I found the controls to the elevator in the floor. I must have pressed them on accident." Cass flipped up the carpet and pointed to the row of buttons.

"A forest? As in a bunch of trees?" Grayson raised his eyebrows.

Cass knew it sounded ridiculous, but now wasn't the time to argue. There was a zoo of mutated birds beneath their feet. She nodded. "And a bird talked to me. In English."

Grayson reached out to touch the back of his hand to her forehead. "You're not running a fever."

She batted his hand away. "I'm serious. And not delusional."

"I believe you," the boy said softly. "This place has a lot of secrets."

. "I'm Agent Sparks. Who are you, and how do you know so much about this place?"

The boy put his fists on his hips. "I'm Phineas, and I think whoever is hiding out here took my sister and my dad. I've been trying to find them."

His little face scrunched up with determination. Cass knew there was no convincing the boy to stay behind while she and Gray went back in. She glanced up to Grayson, who shrugged his shoulders. He'd probably already tried to talk the kid out of tagging along.

"Did you call for backup?" she asked Grayson.

He crossed his arms. "Of course. They are a few minutes out. We should wait."

Cass swallowed a shiver that threatened to trickle down her spine. "You didn't see what I saw. There's no telling what this Sandy would do if she knew FUC and ASS were on their way. We need to start the rescue before anything vile happens."

Phineas nodded. His eyes widened. "What did the bird say? The one who talked?" he asked.

"Run."

"Run?" Grayson repeated, exchanging a worried look with her.

"I didn't see any observation room or cells or cages for the victims," Cass continued. "Just the underground forest at the end of the hall,"

"Maybe there's another way down," Phineas hypothesized. "I found feathers at the other mall entrance but couldn't figure out where they went to. There wasn't a trail for me to sniff out."

"Which makes sense if there's another elevator at that entrance," Grayson proposed. Then he turned to look at the boy. "Can you take us there?"

Phineas nodded with a sly smile.

Grayson decided to take his backpack with him in human form in case one of them needed to shift. Especially if it was Cass. He knew she'd rather risk her life than leave her favorite heels behind. Maybe that was a bit of an exaggeration, but she'd be really sad if something happened to them, and Grayson did not want to see an upset Cass. If he could be the hero by carrying them for her, he would.

Cass fiddled with the buttons until she found the one that operated the barrier. In a flash, it rolled up as quickly as it had slammed down on her earlier. They walked in human form through the vestibule back into the dark mall. Cass had left the rug over-turned so that no one accidentally hit one of the controls in the floor. Phineas led them through the building. Dust swirled on the old tiles, clumping in places around old benches and giant pots filled with dead ferns.

"We're almost there." He turned the corner toward another corridor jutting off the main atrium.

It was just past where Grayson first ran into the boy. The entrance shined dimly at the end of the hall as sunlight filtered through the dirty glass.

Grayson held the inner set of glass doors open for the rest of the gang to pass through. They all piled into the vestibule. Cass crouched down to roll up the carpet.

"See," Phineas said pointing to a couple of loose white feathers in the corner.

"We didn't doubt you for a second." Grayson watched Cass search for the controls.

"I don't understand," Cass said, rubbing her hand across the smooth tiles under the carpet.

"Maybe the other way in is supposed to be a trap. That could be why the bird warned you," Grayson mused.

Phineas knelt down with her. "Press on them. Like in the movies. Maybe there's a hidden compartment."

They methodologically took turns pressing on tiles. Grayson was about to give up when the one under Phineas' tiny hands clicked and an edge popped up slightly. "Can you pry it up with your fingers?"

Phineas did as he was instructed. The tile swung up to reveal a control panel similar to the one in the other vestibule.

"Okay, Cass. Which one takes us down?"

"Make sure you're all far enough away from the

walls before I press this." Cass looked up at them. Grayson edged in from the door behind him. Cass seemed satisfied, pressing the round red button in the center. With a loud thud, gears were set into motion, lowering the floor. After a few minutes, the platform ground to a halt.

"The other one has the controls on the wall to open the door," Cass said as she slid her hand along the wall next to her, searching for another hidden panel. One flipped open, and she pressed the only button inside. The walls behind them whooshed open.

Grayson stepped onto the damp concrete. Dim lights recessed in the walls lit the way. Thudding sounded in the distance. It didn't sound mechanical. The rhythm was organic, like someone pounding.

"Look..." Cass pointed. "There's a series of doors up ahead."

"Did the other side look like this?" Grayson asked, keeping his eyes ahead for any possible threats, his senses alert.

"No. There was only the door that led to the forest room." She looked around, inspecting the new surroundings.

The banging grew louder as they neared the doors. Grayson peered inside the tiny window at the top of the nearest door. A giant ostrich with a human head peered back. Grayson's heart hammered in his chest at the image. Was Sandy trying to get her test subjects stuck in various moments of the shift cycle?

"Please tell me you called for backup while you were outside?" Cass asked, peering over his shoulder into the cell. Her voice was barely a whisper, as if her air had been sucked out. She looked back to Grayson with wide eyes.

The captive inside the room opened his mouth. Instead of words, a shrill chirp came out. It would have been comical if it wasn't so horrifying.

"Yes." It took Grayson a moment to find his voice. It had nearly dried up in his throat thinking about the horrors Sandy inflicted upon her victims. "Cass, you and Phineas work on freeing these shifters and get as many of them as you can up in the elevator. Instruct them to wait in the parking lot until FUC and ASS arrive."

"How do we know if they can understand us?" Cass looked back to the mutated person in the locked room, her brow wrinkled in concern.

"Turn into a bird and cluck at them until they do what you need them to. Just get them out of here."

Despite the circumstance, Cass rolled her eyes. "I don't cluck."

"Whatever. Just get them to safety."

Before Grayson disappeared around the corner, Cass called after him. "Be careful. I don't want to see your hound head on a bird body!"

Cass took a deep breath to calm her nerves. Seeing the unnatural mutations was always the hardest part of her job. It was stepping into a horror flick.

She turned to Phineas, putting a reassuring hand on his shoulders and looked into his brilliant blue eyes. "I'm going to release as many people from these cells as I can. I need you to lead them to the elevator and use the controls to send them up to the surface. Some of them might be difficult to look at and may have trouble understanding us. Please be patient with them."

Phineas stood on his tiptoes, trying to see in the door. Being unable to reach the window, he asked, "Is it that bad?"

"This one is. He can't talk, so I'm not sure if he can understand us."

He bit his lip. "I don't think they'll have a hard time understanding we're here to rescue them." Phineas didn't look or sound convinced of his own words. He shuffled on his feet.

"What do you shift into?"

"A mouse," Phineas squeaked. He put his shaking hands in his pockets.

"If you think one of them might hurt you, turn into a mouse and run. Are you still sure you want to help? There's no shame in waiting back at the car."

The poor kid seemed to have been through a lot. Cass would hate for this to traumatize him further.

Phineas narrowed his eyes. "I want to help. I'm just a little scared."

"It's okay to be scared. I am too." Cass turned back to the door and tried the handle. It seemed to be unlocked from the outside. She turned to Phineas. "If we find your sister and dad, they may not be as you remember them." It pained her to break it to the kid, but she wanted him prepared. Sugarcoating things wasn't going to help.

A solemn expression washed over his face. "I understand."

"Are you ready?" He nodded once more, taking a deep breath.

Cass swung open the metal door. The ostrich charged, nearly knocking her over. The yellow bird eyes inside the man's face circled to the boy. He cocked his head to the side, taking Phineas in. "We're here to rescue you," Phineas croaked.

The man's head bobbed as he inched closer to Phineas. He let out a light trill before ruffling up his feathers.

"It's all right," Cass cooed in a soothing voice. "Can you understand me?"

The man shifted his yellow eyes to her, blinking. He let out a small chirp. She took that to mean yes. Thankfully, he wasn't left with a bird brain that couldn't understand human speech, though he was clearly unable to speak himself.

"I'm an ASS agent," she started to explain.

"Don't be so hard on yourself, Agent Sparks," Phineas piped up with a smile. "It's not your fault they're here."

Cass tried her best not to roll her eyes again. "As in Avian Soaring Security, not that I suck as an agent," she clarified. "Phineas here is going to lead you out once I free everyone." The man chirped in agreement.

Cass took that as a good sign to open the next door. She didn't want to put the kid in additional danger. She opened the next door slower than the first. A goose with white plumage flapped its wings at Cass. It ran out on human legs. She let Phineas explain they were there to help. The first bird seemed to trust him easier. She wanted to continue opening the doors slowly to avoid the risk of one of the experiments knocking the child over.

Things seemed to be going smoothly. It was almost too easy. With any luck, they'd come across Phineas' family. He didn't react to the shifters they let out so far, so she assumed he didn't know either of them. She wondered how Grayson's search for Sandy was going. Hopefully luck was on his side too.

13

It was hard leaving the captives in their cells. Grayson didn't like passing their doors knowing they were inside suffering. He kept faith that Cass and Phineas would free them.

He rounded the next corner. This hallway wasn't lined with doors like the others. This one ended at a single door. Maybe this opened to the forest Cass mentioned.

Grayson paused with his fingers wrapped around the handle. He wanted to be ready for anything. He prepared himself for the worst and flung open the shiny, metal door.

A long, skinny room waited for him. His eyes adjusted to the dark. No lights were on. The only brightness wafted through a picture window, opening to the forest. *This must be Sandy's observation room.*

He traversed the chamber to the glass.

"It's beautiful, isn't it?" a husky voice asked behind him.

Grayson turned to watch a slender woman in a button-down shirt and skirt take form out of the shadows in the corner. The artificial sunlight from the adjacent area lit up the delicate features of her face. If Grayson didn't know better, this woman would have been a realtor, not an evil scientist. He expected an ugly person in a lab coat.

He decided to play along and stroke her ego. "I can't imagine how you created all this down here." An unfelt breeze fluttered the green leaves of the twelve-foot birch tree right outside the window.

"I wanted them to be comfortable."

"Who?"

"My creations."

So this woman fancies herself a god?

"Help me to understand." He tried his best to keep his disgust hidden. He wanted to find out as much as he could. Were there other locations? Was she working with anyone? He didn't want to risk there being more shifters in need if Sandy wasn't feeling generous with her information later.

"Have you ever wanted to talk in your animal form? Some of my creatures can. What about seeing what would occur if one only shifted a portion of their body?" She walked to the window, inspecting the underground world she created. "What others consider demented, I made normal." She smiled wide, proud of the work she'd accomplished.

The light from the window lit up more of her body, exposing long claw marks down her bare legs. From Ellie. His cadet had told him after she was snagged in the talons of the giant hawk that she'd shifted her hands to cat claws and raked them down the bird's legs. This was indeed the red-tailed hawk they were after. He assumed it was also Sandy.

"Do you have more forests like this? More... creations than what is on-site here?" He barely got the words out through snarling teeth. He wanted to grab this bird by the neck and shake like a good dog. He wanted to scream at her for doing this without the permission of her subjects.

She shook her head. "Sadly, my other compounds have been... compromised."

"What did you want with Ellie? The cat shifter?"

Her face contorted as she worked to remember. "The shadow cat. She was most interesting. She didn't get away without leaving her mark on me." She glanced down to the white scars running down her slender legs. "Dr. Smith had his eye on her. You'd have to ask him... oh wait, you FUC agents killed him!" Without warning, Sandy launched herself at Grayson. The light caught on the long knife in her hand.

Grayson barely had time to react before a giant gray bird launched itself into the room, grabbing

Sandy's extended wrist in its giant beak. Sandy screamed. Grayson fumbled around, looking for a light switch. He flicked the toggle to find Peahen Cass sitting on top of Sandy. Cass pinned the tiny woman to the ground, nearly suffocating her with her silky tail feathers. She was nearly sitting on her face. Cass held her long, graceful neck in the air, clearly pleased with herself. The more Sandy squirmed, the more Cass ruffled her plumage to keep her at bay.

Grayson was about to thank her when an army of FUC and ASS agents entered the room. Agent Brett Kipp sauntered in, touting a pair of cuffs for Sandy. He and his girlfriend, Ellie, could rest soundly knowing the hawk that tried to cat-nap her was finally apprehended.

Agent Kipp had to coax Cass off of the bird shifter. She seemed pretty content to have the woman smothered by her feathers all night. She eventually stood as Agent Kipp slapped the cuffs on Sandy. The woman touted a mouth full of large, grey feathers.

Cass transitioned back to her human form as Sandy was escorted out of the observation chamber. "I hope you choke on them!" she shouted at the hawk shifter as she disappeared out of the room.

Grayson chuckled. "You couldn't let her leave without saying something?"

"Damn straight. Words are my best weapon."

"Aside from your beak." Cass nodded. Grayson looked around. "Where's Phineas?"

Cass sighed, wrapping her arms around her body to keep out the cold air. "We found his sister in one of the last stalls. She looks human, but..." Cass paused, choking back a sniffle.

"But what?"

"She's having a real hard time talking."

"Like the seagulls?"

Cass nodded, her red curls brushing her brown shoulders. "We didn't find his dad though. The last door we tried opened to the forest. Phineas is in there with some agents looking for him."

Cass tossed on her clothes and led Grayson into the forest room. "Where is Phineas?" she asked an agent standing on guard near the entrance. He pointed toward a row of towering pines.

They marched toward where the agent indicated. Sobbing filled the grove. Cass and Grayson sprinted toward the sound, fearing the worst. Her breath hitched in her chest as the beat of her heart thrummed loud in her ears, nearly drowning out the sound. If Sandy killed the kid's father, she'd gladly stuff more feathers down the monster's throat. She caught some of what the hawk explained to Grayson before she lunged at him. The woman was three-shades batty.

They cleared a row of bushy evergreens to see a couple of agents hovering near a shaggy-haired boy and a young woman in a hospital gown. Tears streamed down both their faces. Phineas held a normal-sized black crow in his lap, cradling the creature as if it were a porcelain doll. He stroked its back with his tiny fingers. "It's going to be all right," he whispered.

"Dad," the young woman said. Phineas' sister must have been ten years older than him. Tears cleaned a path through her dirt-streaked cheeks. Her matted head of brown hair leaned on Phineas' small shoulder as she put an arm around him. "Dad," she kept repeating over and over, unable to communicate with more than a word.

The crow opened its beak as if to caw. Instead, it said, "Gabby. Phin."

Cass could have sworn she saw a tear leak out of the small bird's eye.

***

Cass sat on the corner of Gray's desk as he typed up his report. Phineas' sister, Gabrielle, was declared stable. They left them in the hospital wing of WANC. Gabby couldn't communicate and would need a lengthy rehabilitation period but was otherwise healthy. Joe, the crow, was a more challenging case. They weren't sure what their doctors could accomplish, with him or the other shifters they rescued. It was too soon to know if any of it was reversible.

You wouldn't know that by looking at Phineas though. He was happy just to have his family back. He didn't care that his dad was stuck as a talking bird or that his sister could only utter one word repeatedly when she tried to talk. They left Phin beaming ear to ear, sitting on his sister's hospital bed reciting the harrowing tale of how he'd rescued a FUC and ASS agent from wandering an abandoned mall and helped them rescue all the shifters below.

Cass smiled just thinking about it. They didn't care what shape they were in, as long as they were there. Together. It was beautiful.

"We did good today," she said over Gray's pounding on the keys. He was racing to complete the reports because Cass had promised to make him her homemade eggplant parm. It was a little out of season, but they both decided they needed some comfort food tonight.

"That we did."

"Are you over your fear of birds pecking your eyes out?"

He shook his head. "I'll probably always wear sunglasses around them."

"Did they figure out what that device was? The one the goon pulled on you in the warehouse?" Cass asked, remembering back to the first time she saved Grayson's ass on this mission.

He shook his head. "The techies are still working on that." He finished typing and looked up at her. "You ready?"

She hopped off the desk and walked around to him, leaning in to plant a warm kiss on his lips. It was a promise of what dessert would be like. "Let's go home, Agent Stone, so I can get you out of these clothes."

EPILOGUE

Gabby leaned back on her hospital bed, trying to get some sleep. Phineas had left hours ago. Her mom was notified once they arrived at WANC and came to get him. She visited for a while before asking a nurse if they could say goodnight to Gabby's father. Her parents were divorced but got along pretty well.

Gabby's mind wouldn't rest. All Phin and the other agents talked about was Sandy, the woman who held her and the others captive. What they didn't know was Gabby saw Sandy's partner. She tried like hell to tell the agents who attempted to question her or the nurse and doctor who performed all sorts of tests on her. All she could get out was the word "no." They reassured her that they weren't going to harm her. They thought she was telling them to stop. They didn't understand she was trying to let them know they were wrong. They were all wrong.

One of the doctors from earlier gave her a notepad. She knew what she wanted to say, but when she gripped the pen, incoherent lines and swirls scrawled across the page.

Gabby pulled the covers up to her chin, trying to fight off the chill from her underground concrete cell. The cold seemed to permanently seep into her bones.

She shut off the bedside lamp, squeezing her eyes shut. If she were to get better, she'd need rest. And as soon as she could talk again, that son-of-a-bitch Dr. Grimm was going down. If she had to fly there on her own dark wings, that bastard was going to pay.

The End

Or is it? Stay tuned for Gabrielle's story, coming soon in Birds of a Feather *by Scarlet Fox!*

And there are more FUC Academy books from other authors coming your way!

To find out more about these books and more, visit worlds.EveLanglais.com or sign up for the EveL Worlds newsletter. If you haven't already downloaded the **free Academy intro** (written by Eve Langlais) make sure you grab it at worlds.evelanglais.com/wordpress/book/fucacademy1!

Taming the Tiger

After being rescued from experimentation at a lab, Paige wants nothing more than to get on with her life. What's more frustrating than trying to fill in the blanks of her memory is the annoying—yet sexy—FUC agent who is hell-bent on protecting her while finding those responsible for her condition. But this tiger is sick of being kept in a cage.

Troubling memories from Jake's past leave him obsessed with arresting those who held Paige in captivity. If his nagging desire to be closer to her didn't prevent him from spending all hours of the day on the case, Jake is sure he would have outfoxed the evil scientists by now. But something keeps leading him back to Paige.

Can Jake keep his focus long enough to find those responsible for the atrocities committed against Paige? Or will a major miscalculation allow them to find her and complete their experiment?

<u>Available on all major platforms!</u>

Shadow Cat and the Sloth

A great outdoors adventure might be more than this cat and sloth bargained for.

Ellie Talbot is a cadet at FUCN'A after being rescued from an experimental lab. She was once human and now can shift into a black cat. Oh, and she can also bend light waves around her to turn herself invisible. NBD.

The shadow cat is thrilled to hear that her technical

training class will be in the field for survivalist training…
until she hears who she's assigned to partner with.

Brett Kipp's sweet sloth smile is nothing short of a ray of
sunshine, but that doesn't help Ellie's confidence in his
survival abilities. Add in the fact that part of their training
includes river rapids, and this trip is no longer the cat's
meow.

Available on all major platforms!

ABOUT THE AUTHOR

Scarlet Fox (aka B.L. Carroll) enjoys writing when she isn't at her day job. Creating romances is a fun challenge for her. Scarlet's alter ego loves writing mysteries and supernatural thrillers with a strong female lead. Destigmatizing mental health and other internal struggles are recurring themes in her fiction. Other hobbies include painting, singing, or going for walks. Coffee is a necessity, as is reading. She lives in western New York with her fur babies and partner.

Please visit her website for other titles and information. Thank you for reading!

Website: scarletfoxauthor.wixsite.com/website

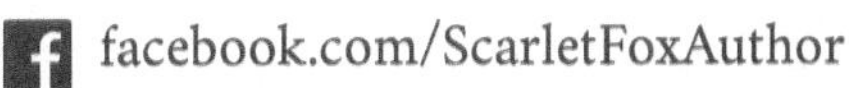 facebook.com/ScarletFoxAuthor